ED LAW

DALTON'S TREASURE

Complete and Unabridged

LINFORD
Leicester

First published in Great Britain in 2015 by
Robert Hale Limited
London

First Linford Edition
published 2018
by arrangement with
Robert Hale
an imprint of The Crowood Press
Wiltshire

A catalogue record for this book is available
from the British Library.

ISBN 978–1–4448–3694–3

Published by
F. A. Thorpe (Publishing)
Anstey, Leicestershire

Set by Words & Graphics Ltd.
Anstey, Leicestershire
Printed and bound in Great Britain by
T. J. International Ltd., Padstow, Cornwall

This book is printed on acid-free paper

DALTON'S TREASURE

After a run of good fortune, Dalton rests up in Sawyer Creek, blissfully unaware of troubles to come. Convinced his good luck won't end, he challenges the crooked Obediah Bryce to a game of cards — and, just like that, loses everything. Forced out by Marshal Walsh and imprisoned in the ghost town of Randall's Point, Dalton patiently plots revenge. Surrounded by enemies, he must trust the unlikeliest of allies if he is to have any hope of escaping Randall's Point and recovering the treasure that is rightfully his.

1

'Your ten dollars, and I'll raise you fifty,' Dalton said.

As the house rules limited raises to ten dollars, the two poker-players who had thrown in their cards groaned, but Dalton's opponent Obediah Bryce licked his lips, suppressing a smile. Then he fingered his chips as he mulled over his response.

They had been playing for two hours and Dalton reckoned he now understood Obediah's reactions, so he expected him to take the bait. More importantly, Dalton had been dealt the best poker-hand he'd ever received and he'd never forgive himself if he didn't risk more.

They were playing two-down, three-up and Dalton was showing a queen and two tens, while his facedown cards were another two queens. Obediah was showing two fives and a jack, suggesting he might have three of a kind or a full house, both of which wouldn't defeat Dalton's superior full house.

The only hand that could defeat Dalton was if Obediah had both fives. After a run of good luck, Dalton didn't feel that his luck would change tonight.

Recently, he had helped out a decent family in the town of Lonetree and he'd been rewarded with five hundred dollars. So he'd abandoned his original plan of heading to Wilson's Crossing in search of work and he'd taken the opportunity to visit Sawyer Creek, a small town with a large saloon.

The Lucky Break saloon provided a safe environment for gamblers, with customers being frisked for guns on entry, the dealers working for the house, and guards on duty to slap down potential trouble. Accordingly, the dealer glanced at the bar and within moments two gun-toting guards approached and stood on either side of the table.

Obediah eyed the men with approval and then picked up a five-dollar chip.

'I understand that the house rules limit raises,' Obediah said, looking at the dealer, 'so I can refuse that raise and call at five dollars?'

'You can,' the dealer said.

Obediah considered Dalton before looking at their cards again. Then he nodded and held up the five-dollar chip.

'In that case I accept your raise; if you'll accept that this chip is now worth fifty dollars.'

Dalton smiled. 'I'll do that.'

Obediah pushed the chip into the pot. Then he stacked up ten more chips and pushed them forward.

'And I'll raise you five hundred dollars.'

Even the dealer groaned at that, but Dalton didn't hesitate for a moment before he matched the bid.

'I'll pay to see what you have,' he said.

Obediah glanced at the gunmen standing on either side of the table as if to remind Dalton not to cause trouble — not that Dalton needed to when Obediah turned over his two cards to reveal two jacks.

'Full house, jacks over fives,' he declared with confidence.

Dalton raised an eyebrow. Then, enjoying the moment, he glanced around taking in the other players, the customers who had stopped their business to watch this hand and, finally, he looked at Obediah.

'That's just about the best hand I've ever seen at the poker-table,' he said. He paused for effect. 'The trouble is — it's not the best one I've ever seen.'

Dalton waited until Obediah gulped and then he flipped over his cards. A gasp went up from the customers while Obediah lowered his head in defeat.

As Dalton dragged the chips towards him, the guards tensed, seemingly more attuned to understanding reactions at the poker-table than Dalton was. Sure enough, when Obediah raised his head he pointed an accusing finger at Dalton.

'I've just been cheated,' he muttered.

Dalton shook his head, but he didn't need to respond when the dealer turned to Obediah.

'I dealt the cards,' he said. 'So if you accuse Dalton of cheating, you're accusing the house.'

The guards moved in to flank Obediah. One man slapped a heavy hand on Obediah's shoulder and bodily dragged him out of his chair while the other man stood back with his gun drawn and aimed at Obediah's chest.

'I'm not accusing the house of cheating,' Obediah shouted as the guard moved to drag him away from the table.

The dealer raised a hand making the guard release Obediah, who righted himself and stood defiantly. He straightened his jacket as he clearly chose his next words carefully.

'I'm an honest man of good standing,

as you can see from my attire, but that man's clothes are dust-caked and trail dirty. I don't reckon he had five hundred dollars to make that bet.'

'Then you shouldn't have accepted his bid,' the dealer said. 'We play with chips for a good reason and the moment you ignored the house rules, you brought this problem on yourself.'

Obediah snorted. 'You should have insisted that he prove he had the money, or else you can't claim that this saloon is a safe place for everyone to play poker.'

To Dalton's surprise several customers murmured in support of this view and with the prevailing opinion starting to sway in Obediah's favour, the dealer raised himself to look at the bar. A message was relayed and a few moments later the owner Virgil Tweed came out from a back room and he was quickly apprised of the situation.

Dalton let the debate play out, figuring that the more people who were involved the worse this would look for Obediah. Presently, Virgil moved around the table to consider Dalton.

'An accusation has been levelled that you made a bet you couldn't cover,' he declared. 'If you can prove that's a lie, the pot is yours and I'll take great pleasure in running your accuser out of town.'

Dalton nodded and stood up. Then, with a fixed smile on his face, he slipped his hand slowly into his inside jacket pocket towards his money.

His smile died when his hand closed on air. He rooted deeper into his pocket and then, feeling foolish, he tapped his other pockets before opening up his jacket.

By the time he'd found the neat hole cut into the bottom of the inside pocket the guards had moved away from the smirking Obediah and were advancing on him.

'Wait!' Dalton shouted, and this time the guards halted and adopted the postures they'd taken when Obediah had been given one chance to explain himself. 'I had five hundred dollars, but I've been robbed.'

Virgil shrugged. 'That's not my problem.'

Dalton thought quickly, but he couldn't think of how he could talk his way out of this situation.

'If I had to prove I had the money, so should he,' Dalton said, offering this lame comment until he could come up with something more persuasive.

Virgil sighed with a weary air and then turned to Obediah.

'If you would be so kind as to comply. Then we can finally end this matter.'

Obediah nodded and, mimicking Dalton's earlier action, he slipped his hand slowly into his inside jacket pocket. Even before the hand emerged, Dalton groaned, knowing what he was about to see.

Sure enough, clutched in Obediah's hand was a wad of bills. It even had the same green string tied in a heavy knot with which Dalton had secured his money before he'd come into the saloon.

He couldn't remember seeing Obediah before he'd met him at the poker-table, but then again a skilled thief only needed a moment to separate a man from his money. Dalton figured he'd struggle to convince Virgil of what had happened and so, before turning to the door, he limited himself to giving Obediah a warning glare that promised him this matter wasn't over.

The guards moved in to flank him and ensure he left, but Obediah hadn't finished with the humiliation.

'I had the money to cover my bet, but he hadn't,' he shouted after him. 'That means he still owes me five hundred dollars.'

Dalton stomped to a halt and stared straight ahead at the door. His mind remained blank for a way to argue his way out of the situation and, with his anger rising by the moment, he whirled round.

Both guards lunged for him, but their

hands only brushed Dalton's back as he broke into a run. He took two long strides and leapt onto the poker-table before launching himself at Obediah.

His outstretched arms grabbed the trickster around the shoulders before both men went tumbling to the floor. They slid along the floor, scattering customers in their wake before they turned a half-circle and fetched up against the bar.

Dalton got in two short-armed punches to Obediah's stomach. Then he raised himself and delivered a satisfying uppercut to Obediah's chin that made his head thud back against the bar, but then the guards pounced on him.

He shook the first man off and then came up quickly to hammer his shoulders into the second man's stomach. He lifted him off the floor and let him tumble off his back. Then he swung round towards Obediah, aiming to mete out some more punishment before he was overwhelmed.

Obediah was crawling away and Dalton advanced on him, but then several new guards came at him from all directions. One man shoved him in the side, knocking him to his knees while two other men secured his arms behind his back.

Dalton struggled without effect, but when they pulled him to his feet he made the guards fight for every step as they dragged him away. Their efforts knocked over the table and barged customers aside, adding to the consternation, but inexorably he was dragged on.

Five paces from the door a newcomer came into the saloon, making the guards stop. Dalton noted the star on the man's jacket and he sighed with relief, assuming that this was the town marshal Brett Walsh.

'Marshal,' he said, 'I've been cheated, robbed, and then cheated some more.'

Walsh ignored him and looked past him at Virgil.

'What's he done?' he asked.

'He ignored the house rules,' Virgil said.

Walsh nodded. 'What are you planning to do with him?'

'My men are running him out of town.'

'You're not doing that.'

Silence reigned for several seconds giving Dalton hope he'd get a fair hearing.

'I'm pleased I'm finally talking to someone with sense,' he said. 'So I'd welcome the chance to tell my side of the story.'

For several more seconds Walsh continued looking at Virgil before turning his cold gaze on Dalton.

'I've got bad news for you, mister,' he said. 'The only reason Virgil's men aren't running you out of town is because that's my job.'

2

Two men were already sitting in the back of the open wagon awaiting their punishment. Walsh directed Dalton to sit between them and then headed around to the seat at the front.

'Has anyone got anything to say in their defence?' he asked when he'd settled down.

Dalton started to complain, but his two companions spoke over him, their grievances clearly having stewed for longer than his had. The first man claimed he'd only been defending himself after being attacked by several other men, and the second man reckoned he'd been apprehended because the marshal was scared of the men who had robbed him.

Walsh let them speak for a few moments and then raised a hand. After a few more grumbles, both men fell silent.

Walsh pointed at each man in turn. 'I should have mentioned first that if I don't have complete silence, you'll all lose your boots. The next time anyone speaks, you'll all lose your pants. So I ask again: has anyone got anything to say in their defence?'

Walsh put a hand to his ear and waited. Wisely, everyone stayed quiet, making him smile.

'Well, if you're not going to explain yourselves, I'd better run you out of town.'

Walsh shook the reins and, as they moved off, the three men in the back stayed silent although they exchanged aggrieved glances.

The first man had cuts and scuffed marks on his face, and he was rubbing his ribs ruefully, suggesting that he'd come off worst in the fight he'd been involved in. The fact that nobody else had been apprehended for the incident gave credence to his claim that he'd been on the receiving end of some rough justice.

The second man was portly and he sat hunched over looking at the other two men with scared eyes. His nervous manner suggested he hadn't caused any trouble, but he had sure been on the receiving end of some.

They trundled on into the darkness, after a few miles joining the creek that gave the town its name, after which they rode along beside the water. Although the three men heeded the marshal's warning, with shrugs, hand gestures and mouthed comments they exchanged opinions among themselves.

Dalton gleaned his companions were Lawrence Jervis and Abraham Shaw. Lawrence had no idea where they would be taken while Abraham did know — and the prospect terrified him.

Abraham's mounting apprehension made the other two men adopt his posture of sitting hunched in the wagon, but his nervousness did at least let them know they were approaching their destination. So Dalton was prepared when a building emerged from out of the darkness.

When Walsh drew up, Dalton raised himself and saw rail tracks stretching away to either side, showing that they had stopped before a station house.

'Randall's Point,' Walsh declared. 'The town here was abandoned last year and the train only stops to take on water from the creek, but nobody will complain when you ride the rails.'

'You can't just leave us here,' Dalton said.

'Quit complaining! You're luckier than some I've left here. The train comes every other day, but the next one is due tomorrow morning. Get on it and don't ever come back to Sawyer Creek.'

'Except I have to! I got robbed back in your town and I reckon so did Abraham, and Lawrence got beaten for no good reason.'

Lawrence murmured that this was the case while Abraham cast sideways glances at the dark station house.

'Be thankful that I've dumped you somewhere where you can move on easily.' Walsh chuckled. 'But if you ever show your face in my town again, I won't be so lenient. I'll stand back and let Virgil's men take care of you. They aren't as soft-hearted as I am.'

Walsh tipped his hat and with it being clear that complaining wouldn't help them, Dalton and the others clambered down from the wagon. When they moved aside, Walsh wasted no time before turning the wagon in a short arc and then trundling away into the darkness back towards Sawyer's Creek.

The sky was overcast, but the moon was up and providing enough illumination to allow Dalton to see that the station house was derelict and lacking a roof. So, unless the other buildings were in a better condition, they faced an uncomfortable and cold night.

He and Lawrence moved across the tracks, but Abraham stayed where he was.

'Come on,' Lawrence said. 'We need to talk and plan what we're doing next.'

'I'm not going no further,' Abraham said.

Lawrence waved an exasperated hand at him.

'If you want to stand around in the cold, that's your choice.' He clambered up on to the platform and got Dalton's attention. 'I don't, so let's find somewhere to rest up.'

Dalton nodded and they moved on, but then his earlier thought that Abraham knew where they were being taken came back to him and he turned round. Abraham was still where they'd left him, but now he was using jerking movements of the head and body as he attempted the impossible of looking in all directions at once.

'Do you know more about this place than we do?' Dalton called.

Abraham didn't reply immediately, but he stopped his frantic movements to stare at a spot down the tracks. Then with a shiver he appeared to accept he'd be safer with the two men than alone, so he scurried across the tracks and then on to the platform.

'I sure do,' he said, his voice high-pitched and petrified. 'Randall's Point is a real ghost town. It's haunted.'

'Haunted?' Dalton and Lawrence said together.

'It sure is,' Abraham declared, seemingly having failed to hear both men's incredulous tones. 'Nobody who has ever come here has ever returned to Sawyer Creek.'

Abraham's eyes were wide and staring and, despite his obvious fear, Dalton couldn't help but laugh. Lawrence then laughed, but Abraham ignored them and returned to glancing around frantically.

'Calm down, Abraham,' Dalton said. He slapped both hands on his shoulders and tried to hold him steady, but that made Abraham flinch as if he'd been shot. 'It's an obvious point to make, but perhaps people don't ever return to Sawyer Creek because the marshal warned them off.'

'It's not just that. People have seen things here that don't make no sense and they've heard terrible screams in the night that couldn't have been made by no living man.'

'These would be people who came here and saw and heard these scary things, and then returned to Sawyer Creek to tell everyone about how nobody who has ever come here gets to return?'

'That's right.'

Dalton waited for Abraham to note the major flaw in his argument, but if anything Abraham had spooked himself even more and he started trembling.

'You need to take your mind off the things those people have told you.' Dalton put an arm around Abraham's shoulders to shepherd him to the station house while casting Lawrence a glance that asked him to resist the urge to make fun of him. 'So, tell us what happened to you.'

In a faltering voice Abraham described

an incident in which he'd been forced to sell his horse to pay a debt incurred in the Lucky Break saloon. But his horse had gone missing and so had all his property. Walsh hadn't accepted his story, but he had deemed the unpaid debt important enough to send him here.

Lawrence provided a supportive groan and then described how he'd been thrown out of the Lucky Break saloon earlier in the evening after arguing with another customer. He'd been followed out of the saloon by several men who had administered a beating.

As with Abraham, Walsh had viewed Lawrence to be the one at fault. Dalton then provided his story, making both men nod.

The similarity of their hard-luck stories depressed Dalton, but their conversation appeared to take Abraham's mind off his immediate fear as he stopped trembling and constantly looking around.

They explored the derelict station

house, finding nothing of interest. Only one corner was robust enough to shelter them from the wind, so they moved on in search of somewhere more hospitable. Unfortunately, there were only another five derelict buildings on either side of a short main drag, and from the outside none of them showed any obvious signs of recent habitation.

'Randall's Point sure is a ghost town,' Lawrence said, and then flinched when he realized what he'd said. But Abraham didn't appear to have heard him as he peered at the building facing them.

Dalton noted this was the most substantial building in town, looking as if it had once been a stable.

'We should seek shelter there,' Dalton said, getting a grunt of support from Lawrence. 'Which will then only leave us with the question of what we do next.'

Lawrence sighed. 'I hate accepting being beaten for no good reason, but I reckon going back to Sawyer Creek won't get me nothing other than another beating. I'll move on tomorrow.'

'I agree with the sentiment, but Obediah Bryce stole my money and I had to leave behind everything I owned.'

'So did I, but the way I look at it, we didn't lose everything. We're still alive and, from what Abraham said, it sounds as if nobody risks returning to Sawyer Creek.'

The mention of his name made Abraham turn to them.

'They can't return,' he said. 'They all die here.'

Dalton frowned, now bored with Abraham's ravings.

'Perhaps it will be too risky to return to town unarmed,' he said, ignoring Abraham. 'But the way I figure it, Obediah can't stay in town for ever. When he leaves, I'll be waiting for him.'

Lawrence nodded, but Abraham backed away for a pace, barging into both men. He didn't appear to notice as he pointed at a building on the edge of town.

'You won't get to find that man,' he said, gloomily. 'We're all about to die.'

Abraham continued to back away, making both men move aside. Dalton narrowed his eyes as he peered into the gloom, trying to see what had spooked Abraham.

It may have been a trick played by the poor light, but beside the building that had worried Abraham something was moving, although it didn't appear large enough to be human. As Abraham moved away from them, he turned to Lawrence, who stared at the building until he snorted a laugh.

'That's no ghost,' he said. 'A rag's caught on a dangling piece of timber and it's flapping in the wind.'

Dalton joined Lawrence in laughing, but Abraham dismissed the explanation with a muttered oath. Then he turned on his heel and hightailed it away across the main drag. They watched him until he skirted around the station house.

'I wonder,' Dalton said, 'if he'll be joining you tomorrow when — '

Dalton broke off when an agonized scream rent the air coming from behind the station house. No matter how spooked Abraham had been, Dalton wouldn't have expected him to make that much noise.

He and Lawrence broke into a run and they were ten paces from the spot where Abraham had disappeared from view when Abraham came back around the corner of the station house.

Both hands clutched his stomach and his mouth was wide open. He took a pace towards them and then stopped.

'I told you,' he said, gasping out each word. Then he keeled over.

The movement revealed the spike that was sticking out of his back. When Abraham hit the ground and rolled to the side, Dalton saw that the bar had been driven all the way through his body leaving two feet of metal protruding out of both sides.

Abraham twitched once and then

stilled, making Dalton accept there was nothing they could do for him, but he moved forward cautiously while looking at the corner of the building. Then Lawrence got his attention with a murmured grunt of alarm.

Dalton turned round to see that earlier Lawrence had been wrong in identifying the movement on the edge of town as being a rag. He could now see that a man was walking towards them, while from beside other buildings more men were coming into view.

The men moved into the centre of the main drag, their forms just hulking outlines in the poor light. When they came closer stray twinkles of light gleamed off the variety of weapons they were brandishing.

They were armed with knives and metal bars, and their intention was clearly to herd Dalton and Lawrence towards the station house. When Dalton had turned fully around, the man who had killed Abraham arrived.

He planted a foot on Abraham's back

and with a sickening lunge he dragged the spike out of his body. Then he advanced on them while swishing the spike, sending glistening globules of red showering from side to side.

'Any ideas?' Dalton asked as he joined Lawrence in backing away from the killer.

'Abraham had the right idea,' Lawrence said. 'Run!'

Dalton turned hurriedly on the spot, but they were almost surrounded. The only route now to possible safety would require them to run past a number of buildings, suggesting these paths were being kept open because other men were lying in wait in the darkness.

'Running won't help us,' Dalton said. 'So we fight.'

3

Lawrence moved to stand behind Dalton's back where he faced the men advancing down the main drag, leaving Dalton to face the man brandishing the spike.

'I don't reckon any of them have guns,' Lawrence said. 'So we need to get a weapon off one of them and then we might be able to break through.'

'Forget about running,' Dalton said. 'These people thrive on fear, so we just have to work out which one is the leader and we go for him.'

Lawrence grunted with approval of this plan, but before Dalton could start working out who their leader might be, the surrounding men came charging towards them. Dalton didn't see who gave the order to attack, but he put that concern from his mind and moved on to confront the spike-wielding man.

The man drew back his arm to swing the metal spike at Dalton's head, so Dalton rushed in, seemingly oblivious to the danger. The moment he came within his opponent's range, the spike came hurtling round, but Dalton expertly ducked beneath it.

While the bar sliced through the air above his shoulders, he thudded a low punch into his opponent's side and then moved on. He heard a grunt of effort as the man attempted a second swipe at him, and so he turned round quickly to find his opponent off-balance with the end of the spike resting on the ground after his ineffective lunge.

Dalton took two long paces and hammered a punch into the man's cheek that made him stumble to the side, and then followed through with a second punch that bent him double. The man didn't fight back, taking the punches with grim resilience, and so Dalton hurled back his fist, aiming to flatten him with a haymaker of a punch.

A moment before he launched the

punch he registered the malevolent gleam in the man's eyes and he checked his intended blow while raising his other hand. His foresight paid dividends when the man raised the spike and jabbed it forward, aiming to skewer Dalton, perhaps in the same way that he'd killed Abraham.

Dalton arched his back while dancing back for a pace, letting the bar whistle past his chest and then, with only a short movement of the arms, he grabbed the spike. The slick metal slipped through his fingers until his left hand fetched up against his opponent's hand.

He gathered a hold of the spike with one hand and, after a moment spent feeling the metal with his other hand, he found a dry spot. Then, with both men gripping the spike using two hands, they strained for supremacy.

His opponent kicked at Dalton's ankles, trying to knock Dalton over while Dalton shoved forward, trying to push the man over on to his back. Both attempts failed.

Dalton stayed far enough back for his opponent's intended blows to only kick dirt while his assailant had planted one foot firmly on the ground and Dalton couldn't tip him over. Their scrambling efforts while gripping the spike between them moved Dalton to the side, letting him see how Lawrence was faring.

Five men were surrounding him, but he had secured a knife from a man who was now lying on the ground. Lawrence was swishing the knife from side to side while crouching forward, seeking to deter anyone from moving in.

Even as Dalton watched, one man stepped forward, drawing Lawrence closer, but that had been only a feint and he moved away quickly as another man came at Lawrence from behind. Lawrence was aware of the potential attack as he spun on a heel and slashed at the man's side, forcing his attacker to scramble away hastily.

The rest of the group edged back for

a pace and after his initial success Lawrence snarled at them. Heartened by Lawrence's determined defence, Dalton locked his arms and drove forward.

His opponent countered, putting so much effort into his attempt to dislodge the spike from Dalton's hands that spit drooled from the corner of his mouth. They strained without moving, but then from the corner of his eye Dalton saw two men make a coordinated assault on Lawrence, who managed a wild slash with the knife and a punch before they bundled him to the ground.

With Dalton distracted, his assailant took advantage and twisted the spike to the side. Dalton tried to counter, but both his hands moved along the metal for a few inches and they met a slick length, making him lose his grip.

The spike went hurtling to the side clearly with greater speed than his opponent had expected as he followed it. The spike jabbed down into the ground with the man standing bent over beside it.

Quickly, before the man could recover, Dalton kicked out. His raised foot hit the spike high up, making it pivot down and thud into the man's forehead.

The man went down on his rump, leaving the spike still impaled in the ground and so Dalton followed through with a second kick that crunched into the man's chin, poleaxing him. Dalton yanked the spike from the ground and turned to Lawrence's fight, where he found that his colleague had already been overcome.

Two men were holding him down with one man sitting on his chest and the other man clutching the knife that Lawrence had been brandishing earlier. They were not paying attention to Dalton's fight and with a slow and cruel movement the knife-wielder brought the knife down towards Lawrence's neck.

Lawrence strained to move away

from the knife, but he was being held firmly and, with only moments to act, Dalton swung back the spike, aiming to hurl it at Lawrence's assailants. Then he stayed his hand and converted the motion into one in which he swung the spike round to hold it over his defeated adversary's neck.

'Wait!' he shouted. 'Kill him and I'll kill your leader.'

Dalton did not know if he had made a correct assumption, but the group of men swung round to face him. The man holding the knife tensed as he weighed up the situation and then moved the weapon so that the point was aimed at Lawrence's neck, mimicking Dalton's threat.

'Do that and your friend dies a moment before you do,' he snarled.

The group of men spread apart, but they didn't come any closer, giving Dalton heart that he had rattled them.

'I know that you'll try, but it won't happen because you won't force me to spike him. You'll all back away.'

Everyone glanced at each other, their slowness in making a decision reinforcing Dalton's opinion that he had captured their leader. With nobody making an aggressive move, the supine man stirred.

'Just do what he says,' he said, groggily.

With that, Lawrence bucked the man sitting on his chest, who didn't resist letting Lawrence scramble away from under him. Then he secured his assailant's knife without trouble and hurried along to join Dalton.

By this time the men were backing away and so Dalton and Lawrence combined forces to ensure the stand-off developed in their favour. Lawrence took over the duty of threatening their captive by holding the knife to his neck while Dalton dragged the man to his feet and secured him from behind with the spike held across his chest.

'Who are you?' Dalton asked, as the men continued to back away.

'I'm Cyrus McCoy,' the man said,

'and these are my trusted men.'

'Why did you attack us?'

'Anyone who comes here is ripe pickings.'

'Then you'd have been disappointed. We were thrown out of Sawyer Creek with only the clothes we were wearing.'

Cyrus shrugged. 'To men who have nothing, you have plenty.'

'You're well-clothed, you have weapons — you don't look starving to me.'

'That's because we scavenge from the train, too. We're no threat to nobody who's not a threat to us.'

'We were no threat to you.'

'Everyone who comes here is either with us or against us.'

Dalton couldn't think of an appropriate reply to someone who responded so aggressively to any comment and so, when Cyrus's men had melted into the darkness, he escorted him away. Dalton figured they would have to find somewhere to hole up until the train arrived, and so the station house was the most convenient place.

Even so, he didn't welcome the prospect of keeping Cyrus's men at bay until then with their only advantage being their hostage. When they reached the station house, they stood in the doorway and in the poor light Dalton searched for a secure position they could defend.

Lawrence considered their prisoner and then moved round to face him.

'Are you saying that Marshal Walsh once ran you scavengers out of town?' he asked.

'Sure,' Cyrus said. 'He told us to leave on the train and never return to Sawyer Creek. We did one of those, except he doesn't know we're still here.'

'Some people have worked out that something is amiss out here. The man you killed had heard rumours that this place is haunted.'

'Why do you think we killed him?' Cyrus laughed. 'We have everywhere in town. We heard him talking. He can't go spreading rumours like that.'

Lawrence gripped his knife tightly, looking as if he'd jab the point into Cyrus's neck. But, as if suddenly changing his mind, he jerked the knife away and turned to look down the main drag. When his consideration of the quiet town reached Abraham's hunched-over body he shook his head sadly and turned back to Dalton.

'This place is open and we can see anyone coming,' he said. 'But prevailing won't be easy.'

Dalton nodded and raised the metal spike to hold it across Cyrus's throat. He looked again at the interior of the derelict station house, not relishing what the rest of the night would bring.

In a sudden decision he swung the spike away from Cyrus's neck and pushed him aside.

'It won't,' he said. 'So we'll try something else.'

'You want to let him go?' Lawrence asked.

Cyrus murmured the same sort of question while fingering his throat, but then he nodded knowingly, suggesting to Dalton that this might be their only option that would work.

'It seems only fair after they let you go.' Dalton said, and then turned to Cyrus. 'We're not threatening you now. All we want is to leave this place, but if you come for us again, we'll more than threaten you.'

Cyrus walked up to Dalton, his face set in a sneer, making Lawrence tense, but Dalton didn't react and, after making eye contact with him, Cyrus snorted and turned on his heel.

'Pleasant dreams,' he called as he walked away slowly.

'You reckon that was a good idea?' Lawrence said when Cyrus reached the main drag.

'No,' admitted Dalton, eyeing Cyrus's receding form. 'But if we'd kept him hostage, his men were sure to come. This way there's at least a chance they'll stay away.'

Lawrence sighed. 'So what do we do now?'

Dalton slipped into the station house and picked out the most sheltered corner.

'We do what Cyrus said and have pleasant dreams.'

*　　*　　*

Something nudged Dalton's shoulder, making him come awake suddenly. But to his relief, Lawrence was shaking him and, even better, it was light. They had taken it in turns to sleep while the other man had kept watch, but as it had turned out the night had passed without reprisals.

Dalton joined Lawrence in leaving the station house and they looked along the main drag. Worryingly, in the night Abraham's body had been dragged away without either of them hearing anything, but nobody was visible now.

'Now that you've seen how much trouble is out here,' Lawrence said, 'are you joining me on the train?'

'No, but I'll stay with you until the

train arrives,' Dalton said. 'Then I'm going in search of Obediah Bryce.'

'I know you want to make him pay for what he did to you, but the marshal won't be pleased if he finds you.'

'He won't, but that won't matter none because I plan to find him. Somebody needs to tell him what happens to the people he dumps here. Hopefully, he'll accept my excuse for returning to town and while I'm there, I can settle my differences with Obediah.'

Lawrence nodded and then they reverted to silence as they resigned themselves to waiting. They judged the passage of time from watching the rising sun but, as they didn't know when the train would arrive, time passed slowly.

Dalton judged that the sun was approaching its highest point when Cyrus's men stirred. They moved to the building nearest to the station house, a mercantile.

They disappeared from view quickly, although, when Cyrus arrived he stood beside the platform and tipped his hat to them while smiling. Dalton returned the gesture and then for a long moment Cyrus faced them before he joined his men.

'What do you reckon that meant?' Lawrence asked.

'He was telling us he'll let us leave, but that we're not to warn the train.'

Lawrence shrugged. 'They only scavenge from the train so I guess that's fine, and the more important point is the train must be due.'

A few moments later Dalton caught sight of the approaching engine and so he bade Lawrence good luck. Lawrence returned the sentiment along with handing over his knife, figuring that Dalton had a greater need for it.

As they reckoned there was nothing to be gained by being secretive, they stood openly on the platform. The train didn't carry passengers and aside from two engineers only one other man was on board to guard the freight.

While the engineers dealt with taking

water from the creek, the guard came down and considered them.

'You're the first people who have been waiting here for a while,' he said. 'Marshal Walsh must be keeping Sawyer Creek under control.'

'Either that or someone else is getting to them first,' Dalton said.

Lawrence flashed him a warning glare, but the guard frowned.

'I've always thought that Virgil Tweed was more in control of that town than the marshal was.'

With the guard reaching the wrong conclusion, Dalton said no more and so the guard directed Lawrence to one of the cars. While he slipped inside and slid the door closed, Dalton noted Cyrus's men moving into position to begin their latest scavenging mission.

Two men scurried beneath the train to disappear into hiding on the other side while another man took up a position at the back. When the guard returned, Dalton engaged him in small talk while trying to work a warning into the conversation that would tell him this place was unsafe yet avoiding escalating the situation beyond petty robbery.

He had yet to find a way when a warning cry went up on the other side of town. Dalton wondered if this was a distraction to aid Cyrus's activities, but he saw nobody move near the train and the guard viewed that this was the right time to leave.

He got the engineers' attention and in short order they returned to the train. Dalton couldn't see anyone else making a move and so he assumed Cyrus had abandoned his mission.

The cry came again and this time there was no mistaking that it came from someone in distress. Dalton headed back to the station house. Lawrence's knife was tucked into his belt, but he still collected the spike before he moved on into the main drag.

He could not see anyone and he could not work out where the cry of alarm had come from. Wondering if this was a trap, he began to think that he would be better served in leaving town now, when suddenly a man backed out of an alley between two buildings with his hands raised in a warding-off gesture.

Behind Dalton the train lurched into motion making the man turn around, his brisk motion suggesting he was minded to leave on it. Then he saw Dalton and he came to a sudden halt.

Dalton stopped in surprise, too.

The man was Obediah Bryce.

4

Dalton moved towards Obediah purposefully, making Obediah look over his shoulder at whoever was behind him and then again at the train. The engine had now moved beyond the station house and so Obediah broke into a run, cutting across the main drag and aiming for the endmost car.

Dalton moved to intercept him and as he was nearer to the tracks than Obediah was, Obediah skidded to a halt. Obediah wavered for a moment and then ran diagonally down the main drag aiming for the stable.

Dalton followed him at a cautious pace and so Obediah was twenty paces ahead of him when he rounded the corner of the stable. Dalton took a wider berth to ensure he could see what was ahead and his caution paid off when he found that Obediah had stopped.

Ahead of Obediah stood Cyrus McCoy. He'd gathered up another spike and was brandishing it at Obediah, who looked over his shoulder at Dalton before with a resigned shrug he raised his hands in surrender.

Cyrus laughed and with quick steps he advanced on Obediah and then jerked the spike forward. At the last moment Obediah registered Cyrus's intent and he stepped away while lurching to the side, but he was too slow to avoid the pointed end of the bar hammering into his ribs.

From two feet away both men looked at each other. Cyrus grinned while Obediah leaned forward with his hands rising to clutch the spike.

Then Obediah keeled over sideways to lie curled up, leaving Cyrus gripping the bloodied spike. Cyrus eyed the spike in Dalton's hands and then, in an obvious challenge, he swung the bar up to hold it in two hands as he had done last night when they'd tussled.

'You shouldn't have done that, Cyrus,' Dalton said, advancing on him.

'Have I just killed another friend of yours?' Cyrus asked.

'Nope.' Dalton approached steadily until he was five paces from Obediah, who was keening pitifully as his life blood spilled on to the ground. 'This man was the reason I got run out of town.'

'Then you'll be pleased you got to see him die before I kill you.'

'Our deal last night was to stay out of each other's way.'

'It was, but the train's leaving town — and you're still here!'

Dalton swung the spike hand over hand as he accustomed himself to its weight.

'I bested you last night. I can best you again.'

'Maybe, but today I have the advantage of knowing your weaknesses.'

'As do I yours. I was watching the train and you and your scavengers got 'nothing from it.'

'Maybe that's what it looked like to you and the train guard, but we got three boxes off the train.' Cyrus chuckled. 'We're skilled at sneaking up on people without them noticing.'

Dalton was about to reply. Then he caught the inference in Cyrus's taunt and he stepped to the side while turning, his quick action saving him from the man who had been sneaking up on him from behind with a knife held high.

The man slashed the knife back-handed at Dalton's chest, who in an instinctive reaction sought to parry the knife with the spike. He missed the knife, but he delivered a stinging blow to the man's knuckles, making him cry out while the knife went spinning from his hand.

The man hurried away, but behind him other men who had attacked him last night stepped into view. Dalton brandished the bar two-handed while he moved to put the stable at his back so he could limit the directions from which he could be attacked.

Cyrus stayed where he was while the other men moved round to form an arc around Dalton, ensuring they could block him if he tried to flee. Aside from Cyrus there were six men, three armed with knives and three with cudgels.

They edged towards Dalton slowly while Dalton stood impassively with the spike held before him. He figured that, despite their overwhelming superior numbers, their cautious behaviour would mean they would test him by attacking him one at a time.

Sure enough, the first man to come at him lunged forward with his cudgel and then backed away quickly. Even though Dalton didn't move, he grinned and the second man to come at him carried out the same movement, again without provoking a reaction.

The third man was wielding a knife. When he stepped forward, he crouched down and tossed the weapon from hand to hand.

On the second throw Dalton swiped the bar around and fortuitously caught the knife as it landed in the man's hand, knocking it aside. He followed through with an upwards flick of the spike that clipped the point of the man's chin, cracking his head back and tumbling him over.

'That's enough,' Cyrus muttered. 'Take him!'

The men surged forward and in desperation Dalton swung the bar wildly in an arc. He caught one man's arm a glancing blow and thudded the spike against a second man's chest, but that took all the momentum out of the swing.

Two men joined forces to grab the spike and then yank it from his hands, so Dalton drew the knife from his belt. Even as he raised his hand someone grabbed his wrist and then shoved him backwards while another man ran into his side and bundled him over.

He landed on his knees, losing his knife in the process, but he saw clear space ahead. With only moments to act before he was overcome, he kicked off from the ground and ran.

He managed three paces before someone leapt on his back. He jerked an elbow backwards, dislodging the man, but his assailant still kept a hold of his jacket and by the time he'd freed himself the others had regrouped and cut off his escape route.

Dalton swung round to again put the stable at his back, but he no longer had a weapon and the men facing him were all armed. Then they moved in.

One man swung a cudgel at Dalton's head, forcing him to duck and, as the weapon thudded into the stable wall, Dalton ran at the nearest man. He didn't reach him as someone thrust out a leg, tripping him up and he went all his length.

He twisted over quickly, but it was to find the men had formed a circle around him. None of them moved, but that was only to let Cyrus come closer and, with a cry of triumph, he raised the blood-soaked spike high above his head.

Dalton prepared himself to leap aside, but then a gunshot blasted, making Cyrus tense. Dalton looked around the group, but none of them had a gun and the men must have had the same thought as they all spun round.

Dalton scrambled up to his knees to find that his friend Lawrence Jervis was standing out on the main drag with a gun clutched in two hands and aimed at the group.

'Step away from him or I start firing,' he demanded.

The men ignored his command, so Lawrence advanced, but that only made them turn away from Dalton and edge towards him. With it looking as if they were preparing to rush Lawrence, Dalton got to his feet quickly, barged two men aside, and looked for his knife.

He couldn't see it and, worse, Cyrus raised the spike, clearly planning to hurl it at Lawrence, who was aiming at the nearest man.

'Watch out!' Dalton shouted, making Lawrence flinch and look around the group of men.

Before Lawrence could turn his gun on Cyrus, the group parted to give Cyrus a clear sighting of his target and he hurled the spike. Lawrence was alert enough to leap aside and as he hit the ground, the spike flew past his right shoulder.

The spike stuck down into the ground five yards past him while the men followed through by charging Lawrence, but Lawrence recovered quickly and jerked up his gun, making them check their movement. For long moments the stand-off dragged on until, with a grunt of disgust, Cyrus turned on his heel and broke into a run.

His men followed him and Lawrence hurried them on their way with two quick shots that peppered dirt at their heels. Within moments the men reached the corner of the stable and they ran from view, leaving Dalton to move on and join Lawrence, who removed a second gun from his belt and held it out.

'Take this,' he said.

'Obliged! And I sure am glad to see you again,' Dalton said as he took the offered gun. 'I thought you'd left on the train.'

'I almost did,' Lawrence said with a smile, 'but then I heard the commotion and I figured you'd get involved. As you saved my life last night, I reckoned I should repay you.'

Dalton smiled and then joined Lawrence in hurrying on to the corner of the stable. By now Cyrus's men were scurrying into hiding beyond the last building in town.

Dalton moved to follow them while aiming at their fleeing forms, but Lawrence shook his head.

'Now that we have guns we have to end this quickly,' Dalton said.

'We don't. We have to leave town

quickly. A whole heap of guns was in one of the crates they dragged off the train. They hadn't examined the contents and so I threw the rest of them into the scrub.'

'All the more reason to get to them before they get to the guns.'

'I figure they know this place better than we do and once they work out I got the guns from somewhere they'll go looking for them.'

Dalton conceded Lawrence's view with a nod, but he bade Lawrence to keep a look out for Cyrus while he checked on Obediah. The man was still and Dalton assumed that he was dead, but when he rolled him on to his back, Obediah looked up at him with pained eyes.

'Hurt bad,' he murmured, clutching his bloodied stomach. 'Need help.'

'You are and you do,' Dalton said, 'but you wouldn't hesitate to leave me if our situations were reversed.'

Obediah waved a hand weakly towards a pocket.

'I can pay.'

'With my money!'

Dalton still reclaimed his money and then looked Obediah over while shaking his head. Then, having gained a twinge of satisfaction from Obediah's predicament, he gestured for Lawrence to join him.

'I gather the wounded man's still alive,' Lawrence said while glancing cautiously at the main drag.

'Yeah,' Dalton said. 'So I'll have to try to get him back to Sawyer Creek.'

'I guess that means we will have to try.' Lawrence sighed. 'The next train doesn't come by for another two days and, besides, we have to make sure Abraham is the last one Cyrus kills out here.'

Dalton nodded and then considered Obediah, who was now breathing shallowly and showing no sign that he was aware his fate was being discussed. He doubted that the injured man would be able to walk, never mind cover the dozen or so miles to Sawyer

Creek, so he and Lawrence would have to carry him.

He wondered what they could use to fashion something to move him, and his gaze fell on the spike Cyrus had left and also the spike he'd used to defend himself.

'See if you can find some canvas,' he said. 'Perhaps we can make a stretcher.'

He gathered up the spikes, but when he turned round Lawrence was kneeling down to peer at Obediah.

'Is this the man who cheated you at the poker-table?' he asked.

'Sure,' Dalton nodded. 'What's the problem?'

'He's the man I argued with in the Lucky Break saloon.' Lawrence looked at Dalton until Dalton raised an eyebrow in surprise. 'Then I got thrown out of the saloon and some men followed me. They beat me and the marshal ran me out of town.'

'Two men crossed Obediah and both times the marshal sided with Obediah.' Dalton looked aloft as he considered whether this was a coincidence or connected in some way. He decided on the latter when a thought hit him. 'And perhaps it was even three men?'

Lawrence nodded. 'Abraham incurred a debt in the Lucky Break saloon, but then his property was stolen. He didn't know who took it, but it sounds suspiciously similar to what happened to you.'

Dalton hunkered down on Obediah's other side. Obediah had closed his eyes, either to avoid their questions or because he really was too injured to summon the energy to respond.

Dalton leant over him. 'Sadly, the only way we'll get answers is to get this good-for-nothing varmint back to Sawyer Creek.'

Lawrence grunted that he agreed and, with that, they directed their efforts into making a quick departure. Lawrence had heard Dalton's earlier suggestion after all, as he hurried off to the stable and returned quickly with a huge sack.

'I've got even better news than finding this sack,' he said. 'Obediah came here on a wagon.'

Dalton smiled, but they still used his idea of poking the two spikes through the corners of the sack. They then rolled Obediah onto the stretcher.

Obediah groaned quietly to himself as they carried him to the stable. They were able to hoist him up on to the back of the wagon without difficulty and, even better, the wagon was hitched up and ready to leave, suggesting that Obediah had been ambushed as soon as he had arrived in the deserted settlement.

Dalton took the reins and, with a few back and forth movements, he oriented the wagon to the door and then moved out onto the main drag. Lawrence knelt on the seat so he could look in all directions, but Cyrus and his men had gone to ground, so they wasted no time before trundling out of town.

They headed past the station house and then over the tracks towards the creek. Lawrence pointed out where he had thrown the guns, but the area was between the tracks and the town, and Dalton judged that they should not waste time that Obediah might not have by trying to find the weapons.

Instead, they moved on at a brisk pace beside the creek with Lawrence looking back to town.

'Any sign of trouble?' Dalton asked after ten minutes.

'Nobody has followed us,' Lawrence said, 'but Obediah looks in a bad way.'

As they were far enough away from town that he doubted Cyrus could now attack them, Dalton drew the wagon to a halt.

'Keep watch! I'll see to him!'

Lawrence knelt on the seat and watched out for trouble while Dalton clambered into the back.

Lawrence was right and Obediah didn't look as if he'd survive the journey back to town. He was twitching weakly and murmuring in pain while fresh blood was pooling beneath him.

Dalton opened up Obediah's shirt to reveal the raw wound and then looked around for something to stem the blood loss. Tucked into a corner of the wagon was a bag, which he upturned revealing a shovel, tools, rope, a rolled-up parchment, and a gun.

Seeing few other options, Dalton gathered up the rope and then unfurled the parchment, which turned out to be a painting of a woman reclining on a bed. He smiled and raised it so Lawrence could see, making Lawrence whistle under his breath.

'She must have been important to him if he took her with him.' Lawrence leaned forward when Dalton turned the picture round. 'What was she wearing?'

Dalton considered the painting. 'A smile.'

The picture was a typical saloon-room painting and markings were all over the back so even if Obediah had viewed it as being important, he didn't think it was valuable enough to endanger Obediah's life by not using it.

He folded the picture over, wrapped it around his chest, and then secured it in place with the rope.

When he drew the rope tight, Obediah groaned, but Dalton figured the wrapping had stemmed the blood flow and so he joined Lawrence on the seat at the front of the wagon.

'Hopefully, he'll live until we reach town,' Lawrence said as they moved off.

'And if he doesn't provide us with some answers,' Dalton said, 'then we'll have to kill him all over again.'

Dalton looked over his shoulder at Obediah, who mustered a thin smile, and then he hurried the wagon on.

5

'Will he live?' Dalton asked.

'It could go one of two ways,' Doctor Wainwright said, as he peeled back the wrapping. He considered Obediah's wound and frowned. 'But with the look of that hole, one way is more likely than the other.'

Dalton didn't need to ask for more details and so he and Lawrence backed away across the surgery to give the doctor some room. They had already thought Obediah had died earlier when they had stopped a mile out of town to discuss how they could slip back into Sawyer Creek unseen.

Obediah had been lying still and only when Dalton had climbed into the back of the wagon and shook him had he stirred, and then he'd only murmured quietly before returning to lying still. As blood had soaked through the painting,

Dalton had discarded it and bound his wound with Obediah's own shirt.

As he had worked, he had noted that the wound no longer bled profusely, but he had not thought this was a good sign. While they had ridden into town Obediah had not stirred again, and neither had he acknowledged them as they had carried him from the wagon to the surgery.

Accordingly, they watched Wainwright work while shaking their heads. Then they told the doctor they would be back later to see how Obediah was faring.

The doctor was working intently and he didn't respond, so they moved on to the surgery door where they debated their next actions. They had been lucky so far in getting into town and finding help for Obediah without anyone paying them attention, but Dalton doubted their luck would hold for long.

'I reckon we've got nothing to hide,' Dalton said. 'So we should find the marshal before he finds us.'

Lawrence shook his head. 'It looks as if the marshal threw three men out of town who'd had a run-in with Obediah. There's something going on here, and I don't reckon he'll welcome us asking him what it is.'

Dalton gave a reluctant grunt and then peered outside as he put his thoughts to how they could stay out of sight until they found out if they could get any answers out of Obediah. He had yet to come up with a plan when a shadow fell across the doorway a moment before Marshal Walsh stepped into view.

'Your friend here speaks more sense than you do,' he said, looking at Lawrence. Then he beckoned them to join him in heading to the law office.

Walsh maintained a stern expression until they were all inside. Then he leaned back against his desk and raised an eyebrow, inviting them to explain themselves.

'You'll have already heard some of the reason why we returned to town,'

Dalton said. 'Obediah Bryce headed out to Randall's Point. He got attacked by Cyrus McCoy and a bunch of scavengers who have made the ghost town their home. They killed Abraham and it's yet to be seen if we saved Obediah.'

As Dalton related their tale, Walsh's expression changed from scepticism to surprise. When Dalton finished, he tipped back his hat.

'I ran Cyrus out of town six months ago. I didn't know he'd stayed there.'

'It seems he joined up with other men who reckoned they'd suffered rough justice. If what happened to Abraham was typical, the others who you abandoned there might have been unlucky, too.'

Walsh winced. 'I'll take care of Cyrus before I send anyone else out that way.'

'Be careful. When we came up against them they were armed with knives and clubs, but they might have guns now.'

Walsh nodded. 'I'll bear that in mind,

but before I deal with Cyrus, I have the problem of what I do with you.'

Dalton rubbed his jaw as he considered how best to respond, but the delay let Lawrence air his grievance.

'You heard us talking before so you'll know we reckon you should just do your duty.'

Walsh shrugged. 'I did that when I ran you out of town, but I don't reckon Obediah was behind all your problems. I don't know who stole Abraham's property. It was Virgil Tweed who reckoned you were being aggressive, and it looked as if Dalton here cheated at poker.'

'So you're saying you're siding with Virgil and Obediah, not us, and you're not investigating no further?'

'I'm siding with whoever looked to be in the right, which wasn't you, and I intend to carry out my promise. Now you've returned I'll let Virgil deal with you.' Walsh beckoned them to the window and pointed at a man loitering outside the surgery. 'Your return has already been noted. That's one of Virgil's men and he's watching the law office.'

'One man won't cause us no problems,' Dalton said.

'Virgil himself is standing outside the Lucky Break saloon. Another one of his men is beside the stable and another one has moved out of sight beside the law office.' Walsh smiled and gestured for them to leave. 'I reckon in the next few minutes you'll get all the justice you can cope with.'

Dalton glanced at Lawrence, who gave a resigned shake of the head as he moved for the door, but Dalton stayed to face the marshal.

'I understand you now,' he said. 'You're making it appear you're siding with Virgil, but really you're hoping someone will get riled enough to take him on.'

'Get out of my office,' Walsh said, levelly. 'I have more problems to deal with than you two.'

Dalton smiled, assuming Walsh's lack

of a denial meant he'd been close to the truth. Then he joined Lawrence in moving on to the doorway to survey the scene.

Their arrival made the man standing by the surgery tense and edge forward. Then they saw him nod to someone out of Dalton's line of sight.

'Do we brazen this one out?' Lawrence asked.

'I came back for answers and I've had enough of running,' Dalton said. 'It's time to fight back.'

He looked at Lawrence until he received a supportive grunt in reply and then they moved out on to the boardwalk. He glanced at the four men Walsh had mentioned, noting they had taken up positions that covered the four corners of a rough square.

As Virgil was the most likely man to provide answers, Dalton set off for the saloon. With Lawrence at his side, he walked diagonally across the main drag at a brisk pace.

When they were a few paces off the

boardwalk their direction became clear and so the men to Dalton's left and right peeled away from their positions. As they moved towards them, Lawrence glanced over his shoulder and confirmed the third man was following them away from the law office.

Virgil called into the saloon before moving forward to stand between them and the door.

'What's the plan?' Lawrence asked.

'I don't have one,' Dalton said.

Lawrence laughed. 'That's always the best kind of plan!'

Then he joined Dalton in glaring at Virgil while maintaining a pace that meant the men moving in to intercept them could not reach them before they arrived at the saloon.

'It seems you ignored my warning,' Virgil called when they were ten paces away.

Dalton did not reply immediately as he walked up on to the boardwalk and then kept advancing. At the last moment Virgil registered that Dalton was going to confront him, but by then it was too late.

Dalton grabbed Virgil's elbow and twisted the arm while yanking it up behind his back. Then he slipped behind him to place Virgil before the advancing men, who slowed when they noted this development.

'I reckon you're the one who should heed my warning,' Dalton said in Virgil's ear.

The approaching men moved their hands towards their holsters and so Lawrence stepped up close to Virgil. He used the motion to disguise him drawing his gun and, by the time his action became obvious, he had already pressed the gun into Virgil's side.

A moment later Dalton jabbed his gun into the underside of Virgil's chin. Virgil gestured at his men to stop, although he then turned his head to glare defiantly at Dalton.

'You've only made this harder on yourself,' he muttered. 'Before, you'd have got a beating. Now, you'll wish you'd only got a beating.'

'You've done enough to us already, but we've done nothing to you — yet.'

'Lies like that won't help you and, if he survives whatever misfortune befell him, it won't help your partner Obediah, either.'

'You found out plenty in a short time, but you got the most important detail wrong: Obediah is no friend of ours.'

'I know about everything that happens in my town, and I don't believe you.'

Virgil's irritated tone sounded genuine and so Dalton loosened his grip of Virgil's arm.

'Explain.'

Virgil glanced around. Aside from his men few people were about and so he gestured at the door with his free hand.

'Not out here.'

Dalton released Virgil's arm, but then planted a firm hand on his shoulder. He directed him towards the door by pressing his gun into the small of his back.

'Keep an eye on our friends out here,' he said to Lawrence. 'I'll be back shortly.'

Virgil bristled at his treatment, but with a shrug of his shoulders he gathered as much dignity as he could and let Dalton direct him. At the door he glanced over his shoulder at Dalton's gun arm and, remembering Virgil's policy of not allowing his customers to be armed, Dalton holstered his gun.

Virgil accepted this compromise with a curt nod and they moved on. Inside, only a few customers were nursing drinks at the bar. The fact that they paid them no attention suggested the reason why Virgil had not sought to escalate their confrontation.

Virgil signified that they should head into the room behind the bar where he had been the previous evening when Obediah and Dalton had played poker. The room turned out to be an unoccupied office, so Dalton removed his hand from Virgil's shoulder and closed the door behind them.

Virgil moved on into the centre of the room and spread his hands, as if that answered everything. When Dalton shrugged, Virgil waved an angry hand at the wall behind his desk.

'Are you claiming you had nothing to do with that?' Virgil asked.

'Nothing to do with . . . ?' Dalton trailed off when he saw what had concerned Virgil. An empty picture frame was behind the desk with shreds of canvas showing that a picture had been cut away. 'Are you saying Obediah stole your painting?'

'I'm saying that last night you and he created a diversion so he could sneak into my office and steal it.'

Dalton laughed. 'The woman's smile was that important to you, was it?'

Virgil glared at Dalton, but then he conceded he had a right to be amused with a snorted laugh.

'Of course the picture isn't valuable, but I assume the diversions you,

Obediah and Lawrence created last night didn't last for long enough. So Obediah didn't have enough time to find what he was looking for and he panicked and stole the first thing that came to hand.'

'Obediah created diversions for his own purposes with no help from anyone. All that was on my mind was that he stole my money. All that was on my friend Lawrence's mind was that he got beaten for no good reason.'

Virgil shook his head. 'You two brought Obediah back to town.'

'Only because saving his life is the only way we'll find out the truth. As I promised him, if he lives, we'll make him wish he'd died.'

Virgil looked Dalton up and down and then with a sigh he offered him a thin smile.

'You'll have to get to him before I do.'

Dalton returned the smile. 'I'm pleased we finally understand each other.'

'We don't, but it'd seem only Obediah can confirm your story.' Virgil gestured at the door. 'Stay out of my way, but don't leave town until he has.'

Dalton rubbed his jaw as he considered various choice retorts, but then with a nod he let Virgil make the last threat.

'Until Obediah recovers,' he said levelly, and turned to the door.

When he left the saloon, Dalton collected Lawrence, who was still holding Virgil's men at gunpoint. Lawrence was tense, suggesting the stand-off had been fraught and he accepted Dalton's suggestion that they move on eagerly.

The Double Eagle was the only other saloon in town, and it was a small and quiet establishment situated at the far end of the main drag. They headed there, although Lawrence repeatedly glanced over his shoulder to check they weren't being followed. Only when he'd drunk two whiskeys did he start relaxing.

'What did Virgil say?' Lawrence asked.

'He accused us of working with Obediah to steal from him,' Dalton said. 'I told him we were as much victims as he was, but Virgil was sceptical. In the end the only way we'll prove we weren't in league with Obediah is if Obediah recovers and tells him the truth.'

'Neither of those sound likely.'

'They're not, but even if he dies we still have some hope. The only thing that Obediah stole was that painting, so with luck Virgil isn't as annoyed as he claims he is. As long as we don't cause no more trouble, we might walk away from this unscathed.'

Lawrence sighed with relief. 'So we just have to sit it out and see what develops.'

'We could do that, but I've never liked doing nothing and besides, I reckon we should leave town before Obediah gets his strength back and talks to Virgil.' Dalton waited until

Lawrence raised an intrigued eyebrow and then leaned towards him. 'You see, Virgil has got it into his head that the picture Obediah stole wasn't valuable — except it is.'

Lawrence flinched back while shaking his head.

'That picture of a woman with a smile was no different to plenty of paintings I've seen hanging up in saloons.'

Dalton swirled his whiskey. 'It did seem similar, which is the mistake Virgil made. He was too busy admiring her smile to turn the painting over and see what was on the other side.'

'We threw it away because there's nothing on the other side now except Obediah's blood . . . ' Lawrence frowned and considered his drink as he thought back. 'But if I remember it right, there were some markings scrawled on the back.'

'At the time I didn't look too carefully, either, but I remember there were lines and markings and the outlines of objects.'

Lawrence shrugged. 'You mean like a map?'

'Exactly, and in the centre of that map there was a large cross.'

Lawrence glanced around to check nobody was listening to them.

'So, Obediah stole a map with a cross on it from Virgil's office and went to Randall's Point loaded down with a shovel and other tools.'

'That's the way it looks.' Dalton chuckled. 'And when you get your hands on a map with a cross on it, you're honour-bound to find out what's underneath that cross!'

6

'Are you sure this is where we stopped yesterday?' Lawrence asked, after an hour of fruitless searching.

'We're right beside our wagon tracks, so we're broadly in the right place,' Dalton said. He looked around for familiar landmarks, but when he'd tended to Obediah's injury yesterday he had not paid attention to the terrain. 'I tossed the picture over the side, changed Obediah's dressing, and we moved on.'

Lawrence sighed. 'Then it must have blown away.'

Dalton sighed, unwilling to admit defeat, but when he tried to judge where the wind could have taken the picture and looked further afield, he noted a bigger problem. Two men were watching them, presumably Virgil's men.

Last night they had complied with Virgil's demand to give him a wide berth by spending a quiet night in the Double Eagle saloon. Then they had taken rooms in a cheap hotel where, after getting little sleep the previous night, they'd enjoyed a restful night.

In the morning they had seen the marshal leave town and head towards Randall's Point with two stern-looking deputies, so they had visited the surgery, where the doctor reported that Obediah had survived the night. His surprised expression confirmed that this had been by no means expected, but Obediah was now sleeping and unable to answer questions.

When they left him, one of Virgil's men had watched them leave the surgery, but he had not followed them, confirming that his instructions were to wait for Obediah to regain consciousness. By noon, Dalton and Lawrence were confident that Virgil would honour his offer to do nothing until he had spoken with Obediah, and so they had taken Obediah's wagon out of town to search for the discarded painting.

'We've been here for a while,' Dalton said, pointing out the two men who were loitering on a rise and looking down at them. 'We must be looking suspicious now.'

Lawrence glanced at the men and shrugged.

'Perhaps, but I reckon they're only making sure we don't leave town, and we'll look even more suspicious if we stop looking.'

Dalton agreed with this sentiment, but when he resumed searching he kept one eye on the men. Another half-hour passed before Lawrence got Dalton's attention.

Dalton joined him and noted Lawrence had planted a foot on the blood-stained painting.

'Now we just have to examine it without being noticed.'

Lawrence nodded. 'It looks badly marked, but hopefully there's enough details left.'

Dalton returned to wandering around as if he were still searching. He moved towards the rise, ensuring that the men's attention was on him, and when he returned Lawrence had used the distraction to slip the painting under his jacket.

They headed back to the wagon. When they rode off, Dalton steered a course that passed across the base of the rise and he saluted the watching men, but they ignored him and headed for their horses.

Then they followed them back to town. Lawrence watched the riders until the terrain took them out of sight and then spread the painting out on his lap. He peered at it from various angles as he tried to decipher the markings.

'Is it a map?' Dalton asked as he kept a cautious eye on the scene behind them.

'I reckon so, and it depicts the place we thought and feared it would.' Lawrence turned to him and frowned. 'It's of Randall's Point.'

Dalton considered the markings that were barely visible beneath the encrusted blood, but with Lawrence's help he made out a wavy line that represented the creek and a hill that overlooked the town. Several square shapes represented buildings, with the cross being inside one of them.

Dalton had not spent enough time in town to work out which building this one was, although intriguingly neither the station house nor the rail tracks were marked, suggesting this was an old map.

'We shouldn't worry about returning to Randall's Point unduly,' Dalton said. 'The lawmen will deal with Cyrus and his scavengers.'

'The lawmen haven't returned yet,' Lawrence said. 'Hopefully that means Walsh is now pursuing Cyrus, and if we return to Sawyer Creek to wait for news, Virgil might ask too many questions about what we were looking for out here.'

Dalton considered Lawrence's eager

expression and he had to admit that he wanted to find out what was buried out there without delay, too, but he shook his head.

'I reckon if we double back to Randall's Point now, we'll struggle to throw off the men who are following us, and when we go there to find out what this cross means we don't want distractions. So I reckon we act calmly and choose our moment to sneak away.'

Lawrence provided a resigned nod and with that he slipped the map out of sight. With both men in pensive mood they moved on back to town.

Dalton's hope that a delay on acting on their discovery would avoid drawing unwanted attention to their activities appeared to work as when they sat by the window in the Double Eagle saloon, Virgil's men returned to the Lucky Break saloon.

Dalton reckoned he and Lawrence would struggle to keep their curiosity under control once the lawmen had dealt with Cyrus, but the afternoon passed quietly without the marshal returning. Later, one of Virgil's men hurried into the Lucky Break saloon and he came out quickly with Virgil.

'News about Marshal Walsh?' Lawrence asked.

'No. I reckon Obediah might have woken up.'

Both men winced. If this were true and Obediah told Virgil why he had stolen the painting, they would have to leave town without delay, and so they watched Virgil carefully.

Sure enough, Virgil headed to the surgery. They moved to the door to get a clear view, but as it turned out only two minutes later Virgil came back out of the surgery. The two men watched as he headed back to his saloon at a brisk pace.

'With the speed he came back out I doubt Obediah told him anything,' Lawrence said.

'Hopefully not,' Dalton said, and then beckoned Lawrence to join him in heading to the surgery. 'But if Obediah didn't respond to threats, perhaps he'll respond to encouragement.'

Lawrence gave him a sceptical look, as did Doctor Wainwright a moment later in the surgery, but he didn't object to them speaking to Obediah. The reason soon became apparent when they sat on either side of the sick man's bed. Obediah was paler than the white sheet that had been laid over him and he didn't register their presence at all.

'Perhaps we should wait until later,' Lawrence said.

'He only has to listen,' Dalton said, and then leaned over Obediah to place his mouth beside his ear. 'I reckon Virgil threatened you, which means we could be the only people who can save you from him. Think about that and when we return, tell us what you know about the map on the back of the painting.'

Dalton moved to leave, but Obediah snapped his eyes open to consider him.

'What have you done with it?' he murmured, his voice weak but still

88

conveying surprise.

'I thought that might get your attention,' Dalton said. 'I bound your wound with it and saved your life. With luck it might save your life again.'

Obediah winced. 'If you have the map, you don't need me.'

'We do, because if we're going to return to Randall's Point, we want to know that it'll be worth the risk.'

'It will be.' Obediah looked at both men in turn, his eyes pained but lively. 'What's the deal you're offering?'

'Help us, and we'll get you out of town and away from Virgil's clutches.'

'What assurance do I have?'

'None.' Dalton gave Obediah a stern look and then offered a thin smile. 'Except you should recall that even though you stole everything I had, I got you out of Randall's Point when I could have left you to enjoy Cyrus McCoy's tender care.'

Obediah closed his eyes, exhaustion seemingly getting the better of him, but then he nodded and considered them.

'I needed to distract Virgil to get into his office and so I picked an argument with Lawrence. That failed, so I worked on you.'

'We'd gathered that much, but why were you so eager to get hold of the map?'

'Because it shows the location of Thurmond Bryce's secret treasure hoard.'

'I've never heard of him.' Dalton considered Obediah's greying hair. 'I assume he's your son?'

Obediah nodded and then wheezed several times, but he had only been gathering his strength and he beckoned them to help him lie higher up in the bed. The manoeuvring made him wince, but once he was propped up he appeared more relaxed.

'Tell us in your own time,' Lawrence said, encouragingly.

'I gather that last year Thurmond rode into Randall's Point when everyone was abandoning the town. He bought the saloon because he said he'd always had a hankering to own one. Everyone said he'd fail and they were right. Within a month he was the only person left there.'

'We saw that it's now a ghost town,' Dalton said. 'I doubt any one man could stop that happening.'

'Thurmond reckoned he could and when he failed, he just shrugged and said his only mistake was not to have been ambitious enough. He started afresh on a new site and built the Lucky Break saloon. Nobody thought he'd succeed, but he attracted big gamblers and soon others settled here and the town grew up around the saloon.'

Obediah took deep breaths after his long speech and so Dalton prompted him.

'Where does his treasure come into this?'

'Nobody knew how Thurmond got the money to build the saloon and he got a reputation for covering any bet no matter how large it was.'

Obediah mustered a wan smile

inviting Dalton to fill in the gaps.

'You're saying he bought the saloon in Randall's Point because he knew that a secret treasure hoard had been buried nearby and he used that money to finance his business?'

Obediah nodded. 'We hadn't spoken in years, but he did once tell me he had heard a rumour about buried treasure, and it seems he found it and then used it to make even more money.'

'How did you find out where it was?'

'Apparently, he often pointed at the painting that hung behind the bar, saying the woman in the picture had brought him luck. He said a woman like her was sitting on a fortune, and everyone thought that was a joke. But I knew he was a man who didn't make jokes.'

Obediah glanced away, his troubled eyes suggesting a long history between himself and Thurmond that he would not divulge.

'Your son isn't around no more, so what happened to him?'

Obediah frowned. 'One day Virgil Tweed came here and over a poker-hand playing against the house, the stakes rose ever higher. Virgil wouldn't back down and finally Thurmond bet his saloon.'

Dalton nodded, now seeing where this story was headed.

'And Thurmond lost?'

'No. Thurmond had a full house, fives over tens, while Virgil had only a nine-high straight. But Virgil didn't bat an eyelid. He just claimed that now Thurmond had put a price on his saloon, he'd make him an offer for it. Thurmond accepted and since then Virgil has run the Lucky Break saloon.'

Dalton shot a worried look at Lawrence, who also furrowed his brow before he asked the obvious question.

'I can believe Thurmond built his saloon using money he dug up, but why do you reckon some of it is left?'

'I don't know for sure, but I do know that Thurmond often visited Randall's Point and I reckon that was to collect more money from his secret hoard. After Virgil bought the saloon, he was never seen again.'

'You're saying Virgil had him killed?'

Obediah gulped, his eyes watering. 'That would be likely, wouldn't it?'

Lawrence nodded. 'And presumably Virgil doesn't know about the treasure and he doesn't know you're Thurmond's father?'

'No. My son took after his mother, not me. He was a man with vision and ability. I'm just a card shark.'

Lawrence turned to Dalton. 'What do you reckon?'

'Virgil didn't appear to know that the painting was important or that it had a map on the back,' Dalton said. 'Then again, he's clearly suspicious of our activities.'

Both men turned to Obediah, but with his story told and with the fate of his son presumably on his mind, he was looking drawn, so they helped him to lie back down on the bed.

'Now that you've heard the story,' the

sick man whispered, 'what are you going to do?'

'Virgil's watching us and Marshal Walsh doesn't trust us,' Dalton said. 'So the best plan is to do nothing for a while and let them both relax.'

Lawrence nodded. 'And that'll give the marshal time to deal with Cyrus McCoy.'

Dalton turned to Obediah, who was considering him sternly.

'I didn't mean that,' he said. 'What are you going to do with me?'

'Despite what you did to us, we'll cut you in on whatever we find out there and we'll do what we said and get you away from Virgil. For your part, you need to alleviate his concerns.'

'I reckon I can appear too weak to talk.' Obediah raised his head and flopped it down on the pillow, but when that made both men offer supportive laughs, he raised his head again. 'But remember, if you don't keep your side of the bargain, I can tell him every-thing.'

'We're aware of that,' Dalton said, levelly.

With that agreement made, they left Obediah and sought out the doctor, who considered them benignly.

'I heard plenty of talking going on,' he said. 'Obediah must have enjoyed talking to you more than he enjoyed talking to Virgil.'

'We did all the talking. Obediah was too weak to say a word, and I reckon that'll be the case for a while.'

'Caring for a man that sick will take a lot of my time.' Wainwright looked out the window at the Lucky Break saloon.

Dalton smiled and then withdrew twenty-five dollars from his pocket.

'This should cover his care,' he said, counting the money into Wainwright's hand. Then he added another twenty-five dollars. 'And this is for your trouble in keeping Virgil away from him.'

Wainwright provided a knowing smile and so they moved on. Outside, they made a point of not looking at the Lucky Break saloon as they headed to the Double Eagle saloon.

'If we're lucky, Virgil won't have noticed how long we spent in the surgery,' Lawrence said. Then he pointed out of town. 'And then we just need our luck to continue.'

When Dalton saw what had interested Lawrence, he joined him in stopping outside the law office. The marshal and his two deputies were returning to town, and they were alone.

'You were right about what's been going on at Randall's Point,' Walsh said when he'd pulled up. He dismounted and joined them. 'We found several bodies, all of men I'd once run out of town. But Cyrus had gone to ground and we couldn't flush him out.'

'He clearly knows the town well,' Dalton said. 'But he has to be stopped.'

'I don't need you to explain my job to me. We've just come back to get what we need.'

Walsh smirked, clearly wanting Dalton to ask for more details.

'What's that, exactly?'

'We're resting up for an hour and getting some food and liquor in us. Then we're heading out to Randall's Point armed with dynamite. By sundown we'll have wiped that town off the map.'

7

'Walsh sounded serious in his intent,' Dalton said when the marshal and his deputies had moved into the law office. 'He's going to destroy Randall's Point.'

'And hopefully wipe out Cyrus McCoy in the process,' Lawrence said, 'or at least ensure he's no longer got a hide-out.'

With people milling around outside, both men said no more as they moved on down the main drag. When they reached the Double Eagle saloon too many people were close by, and so Lawrence silently asked the obvious question with a raised eyebrow while Dalton replied with a shrug.

Even if they dared to talk openly, Dalton would not have said much as like Lawrence he had no idea whether whatever was buried in Randall's Point would survive the marshal's planned destruction of the town. One thing was certain though and that was his barely contained curiosity and so, when Lawrence met his gaze and smiled, he returned the smile.

Without discussion they headed to their hotel, but when Lawrence glanced around and reported that nobody was paying them any attention they walked past it. Then they skirted round the back of the buildings to the stable.

Ten minutes later they were riding out of town on Obediah's wagon. They looked straight ahead, trying to avoid drawing attention upon themselves by acting naturally, and hoping that the news of the marshal's plan would be spreading and distracting everyone.

Only when they reached the spot where they'd found the painting did they look back. They saw no sign of anyone following them out of town, so they moved on beside the creek at a brisk pace.

Whenever they had a clear view of the terrain behind, they checked they were still not being followed. But when they caught their first sight of Randall's Point they stopped worrying about what was behind them and concentrated on what was ahead.

They approached using the same route that the marshal had used. This would let them move past the station house with the minimum of fuss and with the maximum chance of remaining unseen, if Cyrus McCoy was still here.

When they'd crossed over the rail tracks Dalton stopped. Lawrence raised himself to survey the scene, and when he reported that he couldn't see anyone in town they moved on.

When they reached the main drag Lawrence used the map to confirm that the marked building was beside the stable and it had once been a saloon, adding further credence to Obediah's tale. The windows and door had been boarded up. Dalton judged it would take them a while to remove the boards and gain access, which decided their next course of action.

Dalton directed the wagon between the stable and saloon, passing over the scene of their last fight with Cyrus McCoy. He pulled the wagon up behind the saloon where he was pleased to see a back door that hadn't been blocked off.

'If we'd stopped on the main drag and Cyrus's still here, he'd have been sure to see us,' he said, 'but there's a chance we won't be noticed back here.'

'I'll keep watch outside,' Lawrence said. 'You check inside.'

Dalton nodded and so, in short order, he jumped down off the wagon and headed to the door. Lawrence took up a position beside the door where he could call to him readily.

The moment Dalton slipped inside the rank odours of human habitation assailed him and so he moved on cautiously, but the short corridor opened up on to the saloon room and it was unoccupied. With his back to the wall he sidled along to the nearest door where he listened. But on hearing nothing he backhanded the door open to find nothing inside other than dust.

He judged that this had once been a store room, and so he moved on to explore the two other rooms. These looked like they had been used as living quarters: the living room was packed with boxes and crates that had presumably been scavenged from the train, while the other room had bedding along the far wall. Dalton returned to the outside door.

'Cyrus holed up in here and he's been using this place to store the things they've stolen,' he said.

'Hopefully, that's good news,' Lawrence said. 'If this is where he usually stays, he must have moved on.'

Dalton smiled at this optimistic take on the discovery and he returned to the saloon room where he stood before the bar. He held the map up to a thin stream of light slipping between two boards in the window and oriented it to the walls.

He judged that the cross had been

placed to the left-hand side of the building where the bar stood. On the other hand, the box on the map that represented this building was as big as his thumb fingernail so he couldn't be confident that the cross marked a specific place in the saloon.

Even so, this felt like a place where something could have remained hidden and so he hurried behind the bar. On his knees he crawled from one end of the bar to the other, but he failed to see any breaks in the floorboards that would indicate a trapdoor.

He stood up and, leaning on the bar, he looked around the saloon room. It contained only a few pieces of broken furniture; nothing untoward — but then again, he shouldn't expect to see anything obvious.

If he could trust Obediah's story, his son had bought this saloon to gain access to treasure buried beneath this building — treasure the owner had never found. Thurmond had then returned to dip into this fortune and since his apparent demise Cyrus McCoy had holed up here, and he also had failed to notice anything untoward.

He roamed around the room, but was unsure what he was looking for and so, after pacing back and forth a dozen times, he hurried off to collect Lawrence.

'We have less than an hour before Walsh arrives,' he warned. 'I'm not going to find it in that hour. I need your help.'

'If I help, Cyrus could sneak up on us,' Lawrence said. 'On the other hand, with Walsh due, if Cyrus does come here, we'll only have to fight him off for a short time.'

Dalton nodded and so they headed to the saloon room where Lawrence considered the scene and then provided a sour look that said he had as little idea about where to look as Dalton had. He did as Dalton had done and considered the map, which led him to face the bar.

Dalton let him work through the problem in his own time and he was glad he had when Lawrence suddenly turned on his heel to face him, sporting a beaming smile. Then he turned the map over to present the painting.

When Lawrence looked at him eagerly, Dalton shrugged.

'I don't see what's excited you,' Dalton said.

Lawrence took the painting behind the bar and looked around until he found a clear spot on the wall where a painting, presumably this one, once stood.

'The picture was on the wall here,' he said. He held the painting up and stepped to one side. 'But perhaps the picture gives us the answer and not the map.'

Lawrence's tone had become uncertain, confirming he had not thought his idea through, but Dalton moved round so he could see the painting and the saloon room.

'The map told Thurmond Bryce that

the treasure was in the saloon some-where, but I agree that he'd have needed more clues to know where in the saloon it was buried.' He pointed. 'The woman is looking over there.'

Lawrence laughed. 'And perhaps she's smiling because she's looking at the hidden treasure!'

Her gaze was set on the door, which did not feel like a promising place to look, but then Dalton remembered something Obediah had told him, and he smiled as broadly as Lawrence had smiled earlier.

'Obediah told us that Thurmond said the woman in the picture was sitting on a fortune, and everyone had assumed it was a joke — except it wasn't!'

Lawrence removed the picture from the wall and considered it. He punched the air with delight and then turned round quickly.

'She's lying on a bed,' he said. 'So we just have to find where that bed is.'

Dalton nodded and then hurried to the last room he had searched. Cyrus and his men had slept in here and so Dalton didn't feel optimistic, but Lawrence appeared undaunted.

Lawrence considered the room and then picked out a cleaner rectangle on the floor where a bed had probably once stood. Several blankets covered some of the floor and when Lawrence kicked them aside he revealed a raised area that looked as if it'd been hammered into the floorboards to reinforce a weak spot.

Dalton and Lawrence knelt down on either side of the area and began experimentally tapping it.

'This is the best possibility so far,' Dalton said.

'And if the treasure is below this spot,' Lawrence said, 'that'll mean Cyrus probably slept over it every night.'

With that thought cheering Dalton, he peered at the raised area, finding a thin gap between it and the floorboards. The light was poor — certainly not good enough to see through the gap

— but when he placed his eye close to it, air blew dust at him making him blink and giving him a feeling that there was space beyond.

'We need Obediah's tools to get under here,' he said.

Without comment Lawrence hurried off and, with the possibility of success spurring them on, Dalton followed him through the saloon. At the outside door they paused, but nobody was visible and so they hurried on to the wagon.

Dalton grabbed the shovel while Lawrence took Obediah's bag. Before returning to the saloon they again looked around cautiously and this time Dalton felt uneasy.

He glanced at Lawrence, who returned a concerned look, and they hunkered down while listening. A few moments later Dalton identified his concern when the sounds of a distant commotion came to him, perhaps of several people moving quickly and approaching the main drag on the other side of the saloon.

'Cyrus or the marshal?' Lawrence asked.

'Whatever the answer,' Dalton said, 'we need to hurry.'

Lawrence nodded and so they jumped down from the wagon and scurried into the saloon. With only a glance at each other they decided their next course of action.

Lawrence took the shovel and placed it on top of the bag of tools. Then he hurried into the back room while Dalton ran to the window. He peered through a gap between two boards and then moved around until he could see most of the main drag.

The situation was as he had feared: two riders were crossing the rail tracks, flanking an open wagon. The low sun was at their backs and so it took Dalton a few moments to confirm that it was the marshal and his two deputies.

He figured this was a better result than Cyrus McCoy arriving and he didn't need to continue watching the lawmen. He called out the good news to Lawrence and when he joined him in the back room, Lawrence had jammed the shovel into the gap and he was trying to prise up the raised area.

He was straining without any discernible effect and so Dalton upended the bag. He rooted through the tools there and picked out a crowbar with a curved end that appeared as if it had been designed for the task in hand.

He moved two paces to Lawrence's side and jammed the crowbar into the gap. Then he joined Lawrence in pushing down.

With his help wood creaked and the gap opened up, encouraging Dalton to strain harder. Then, with a crunch and loud snapping of wood, the raised area flexed up and then thudded down while Lawrence dropped to his knees cursing.

Dalton took a moment to register that it was Lawrence's shovel that had broken under the strain, and not the raised area. He gave his friend a supportive slap on the shoulder before rummaging through the tools again.

While he looked for something else that Lawrence could use, raised voices sounded outside — and they were approaching the saloon. Although he couldn't make out the words, he heard Walsh deliver an order, and a few moments later clattering sounded beyond the front windows.

'It sounds as if we've run out of luck and time,' Lawrence said. 'Walsh's come straight here, which must mean he knows Cyrus made the saloon his base.'

'And so he'll destroy this building first,' Dalton said, completing the thought.

'This is over. We have to let him know we're here and then hope whatever is under here survives.'

Dalton hammered the crowbar on the raised area in frustration before jamming it into the gap again and straining.

'We've still got a few minutes and besides, we need to come up with a good excuse for being here.'

That thought made Lawrence wince. With industrious noises sounding at the front of the saloon as the lawmen presumably worked on laying dynamite, he did a quick circuit of the room as he searched for another way to get beneath the floorboards quickly.

Lawrence's furrowed brow showed the pressure of time was not forcing him to have any good ideas. Then Dalton flinched and looked at the door.

'I don't hear anything,' Lawrence said.

'Neither do I,' Dalton said. 'That's the problem.'

They both cast one last look at the offending section of floorboards and then made for the door. They had reached the saloon room when Walsh uttered a loud cry outside.

Thinking he had just given the order to light the dynamite, both men put their heads down and sprinted for the back door. They had yet to reach the short corridor when the unmistakable rattle of gunfire sounded.

Another volley of gunshots cracked, accompanied by another loud cry.

'Cyrus McCoy,' Lawrence and Dalton said together.

8

With Lawrence hurrying off to check the back door, Dalton risked going to the nearest window. First, he peered downwards.

He noticed a stick of dynamite that had been propped up against a corner post, but it had not been lit and neither had the two other sticks he could see along the front of the saloon. Then he looked further afield.

Walsh and his two deputies were scurrying for cover beside the station house. The position they had chosen gave Dalton a clue as to where Cyrus had launched his assault, and he looked at the abandoned mercantile beside the station house.

Cyrus had gone to ground there prior to scavenging from the train and, sure enough, two of his men were moving to the corner of the building. Although they were too far away for Dalton to be confident of hitting them, they were clearly visible from the main drag, suggesting that they were unaware that Dalton and Lawrence were hiding in the saloon.

Dalton resolved to still his fire until he could take full advantage of the element of surprise. He slipped across the room and informed Lawrence of the situation, and then took up a position behind the window that was nearest to Cyrus's men.

In the short time that he had been away, more of Cyrus's men had revealed their positions and they were now scattered around the mercantile. As Dalton had feared, they were all armed.

Walsh's two deputies hunkered down at the corners of the station house while Walsh slipped into the derelict building. Dalton caught fleeting glimpses of him over low sections of the wall, but he figured he was aiming to take up a position by the door.

'There's no sign of anyone at the back,' Lawrence called as he came into the saloon room. 'I figure I can be more use in here.'

Dalton beckoned him to take the window on the other side of the door and, after some darting around, Lawrence found a position where he could fire through a gap while watching the scene.

'Wait until Cyrus's men get overconfident and make their move,' Dalton said.

Lawrence grunted his agreement. Then they set in to await developments. They didn't have to wait long.

Cyrus came into view for the first time when he led three men in running for the station house. Dalton couldn't see the side wall of the station house and so they moved quickly out of sight, but Cyrus's other men edged forward, confirming they were preparing to attack.

The deputies were aware of the growing danger as they made the first move in edging around their respective corners. Then they loosed off a couple of shots, making Cyrus's men throw themselves to the ground.

That action appeared to be all the encouragement Cyrus needed as rapid gunfire tore out. Unfortunately, the shots were fired on the other side of the station house and Dalton could only judge what was happening from the nervous reaction of the deputy at the far corner who beckoned the other deputy to join him.

That man checked nobody was making a move on his side of the house, and then hurried off. He had covered only half the distance along the wall when the other deputy cried out and keeled over clutching his chest.

His colleague hurried along and went to his knees beside him. A brief shake of the head confirmed he couldn't help him, and then he had problems of his own to deal with when a man came round the corner and loomed over him.

The deputy had enough time to blast

off a quick shot that clattered into the wall and that was enough to spook his assailant into retreating. His success didn't encourage the deputy as he leapt to his feet and pressed his back to the wall while looking to either side as he tried to work out where the next attack would come from.

In the saloon, Dalton slapped the boards over the window in frustration at not being able to help the lawmen. He glanced at Lawrence, who acknowledged with a sorry shake of the head that the situation was dire and they were unlikely to be effective.

Then, without discussion, they took aim at the station house. Both men fired at the building, more in the hope that gunfire from an unexpected direction would worry Cyrus's men into making a mistake rather than to hit anyone.

Their intervention had the opposite effect, making the surviving deputy direct a worried glance at the saloon. Then, presumably thinking that he was surrounded, he blasted off a wild shot at the saloon and then moved on to the gap in the wall that Walsh had used earlier.

He clambered up on to the low wall just as a gunman came round the corner. Dalton and Lawrence fired at this man, but their shots sliced into the wall several feet away from him.

Worse, their intervention did not deter the gunman and he blasted a low shot into the deputy's side, making him double over before tumbling from view into the house. The gunman then looked at the saloon before leaping out of sight.

'Failed again,' Lawrence muttered, unhappily.

'And now we've been spotted,' Dalton said.

Sure enough, a few moments later two gunmen appeared at the corner and peered at the saloon. One man pointed and the other man nodded before they both moved back.

Gunfire rattled and then a gunman

appeared at the other corner of the station house. He faced the saloon and fired two shots at the doorway before moving back.

His action suggested Walsh might have been overcome, but then a ferocious burst of gunfire tore out inside the station house. A moment later, Walsh vaulted over a low stretch of wall.

He fired into the station house and ducked down. With his back to the wall he cast a worried look at the saloon, confirming that news of their presence had spread.

Dalton and Lawrence made their allegiances clear by shooting at the corner where they had last seen the gunman. Walsh nodded and then, heartened, he turned his back on the saloon and moved away from the station house.

He kept his gun trained on the low wall that he had climbed over, so Dalton aimed at the left-hand corner of the house while Lawrence took the right-hand side. When Walsh had covered a quarter of the distance to the saloon, he turned so he could walk sideways, and then he speeded up.

To join them, he would have to skirt around the outside of the saloon where they would no longer be able to cover him, and so Dalton glanced at Lawrence. He was already pulling at the boards over the window, but they didn't move and so, with a grunt, he agreed to head outside through the back door.

Lawrence took only two paces and then muttered in irritation, making Dalton turn around.

A gunman had sneaked into the saloon and was now edging down the short corridor at the back of the saloon room. The moment the man saw that he had been discovered he snapped up his gun arm, but he was a fraction too slow.

Dalton and Lawrence fired at the same time and two gunshots hammered into the man's chest, making him snap upright before he keeled over.

'I'll make sure he's the only one,' Lawrence said, breaking into a run.

The gunfire inside the saloon initiated a volley of gunshots outside, so Dalton turned back to the window. When he peered outside Walsh was running for the saloon while firing over his shoulder.

Dalton picked out a gunman scooting around the right-hand side of the station house and blasted two rapid shots at him. Both shots sliced into the wall before the man, but they did at least make him slide to a halt and duck down.

Dalton took more careful aim at him, but then he noticed where the bigger danger to Walsh would come from. Three gunmen bobbed up over the shortened length of wall and, with calm efficiency, they sighted Walsh.

The lawman was five paces from the saloon. So he stopped firing at Cyrus's men and thrust his head down so he could sprint to safety.

As Walsh sped from view, Dalton

helped him by firing at the low wall. With his first shot he tore lead into the left-hand man's chest, making his head crack back before he dropped.

His shots didn't deter the other two gunmen, who hammered out a rapid volley of shots before ducking down. Dalton fired, but then he had to stop and use valuable moments reloading.

He trained his gun on the station house, but he had only the wall to aim at and nobody emerged. By now Lawrence ought to be outside and in a position to cover Walsh, but he heard no more shooting.

He hoped this meant Walsh had already reached safety, but then the lawman walked back into sight. His stride was faltering and he was clutching his bloodied side.

Walsh stood before the saloon and, with grim defiance, he raised his gun to aim at the station house. Then his strength gave out and he keeled over on to his chest.

Dalton watched him, but he didn't

dare move. So he swung his gun from side to side, aiming along the length of the station house as he waited for someone to show.

Long moments passed in silence. With Dalton not knowing what Lawrence was doing, the feeling grew that Cyrus was now in control of the situation and was already planning his next move.

Dalton figured he shouldn't give him enough time to act and so he turned away from the window. He winced on seeing Lawrence hurry into the saloon, his wide-eyed expression telling Dalton everything he needed to know.

'Surrounded already?' Dalton asked.

'The men attacking the station house weren't the only ones in town.' Lawrence uttered a forlorn sigh. 'It's just us two against around ten men.'

Lawrence hunched his shoulders and kicked at a heap of old rags on the saloon floor. As Dalton watched, the excitement about what they might find here clearly deserted his friend to leave a hollow shell that would rapidly fill with despair.

Dalton knew that in such a state of mind men could give in and find ways to make their worst fears materialize. So he fixed Lawrence with his most confident gaze and walked across the saloon room slowly until he stood before him.

'Then I reckon that's bad news for the ten men!'

Dalton stared at Lawrence until he mustered a thin smile. Then he slapped him on the back and directed him to watch what Cyrus was doing at the front of the saloon while he hurried to the back door.

He glanced outside and confirmed Lawrence had been right and several men were moving into position on either side of the saloon. The sun was about to set and Dalton reckoned his confident comment to Lawrence would hold true if they could hold out until nightfall.

Then they could sneak away from the

saloon under the cover of darkness and, as they knew the lie of the land outside town, they might find somewhere to hole up. So he settled down beside the door where he could shoot at anyone who came too close and then directed Lawrence to do the same on his side of the saloon.

Lawrence nodded and peered through the gap Dalton had been using. He considered the scene and then flinched back.

Lawrence pointed at the boarded door and a moment later a thud sounded. Then the boards peeled away from the doorway on one side.

Lawrence pressed his face close to the boarded window trying to see what Cyrus's men were doing outside, but clearly he wasn't able to see them as he didn't fire.

A second thud made the boards topple over to leave the doorway open. Then someone thrust a gun through the door and fired blindly.

The shots sprayed around the saloon

room, at least confirming that the gunman didn't know where Lawrence and Dalton were. But Dalton reckoned it wouldn't be long before the gunmen came inside. Sure enough, gunfire splattered around the back door with such intensity that Dalton couldn't risk slipping into the doorway to return fire.

In a coordinated move two men came through the front door and hunkered down behind the fallen boards that had come to rest against a table. They both fired at Dalton and, lacking any cover, Dalton could only leap to the floor to lie on his chest.

Neither man noticed Lawrence and he made them pay when he sprayed gunfire at them from the side. Lead hammered into the boards and wall, but one shot caught the nearest gunman with a deadly blow to the neck, making him cry out before he staggered to the side and keeled over.

The second gunman turned to Lawrence while outside another

gunman fired through the doorway. Faced with danger from several directions Lawrence took flight and he skirted around the saloon room with lead hammering into the wall behind his fleeing form.

At the back of the saloon Dalton got up on to his haunches, but he couldn't get a clear sighting of either gunman, so he beckoned Lawrence to join him and make a stand.

Lawrence nodded and so Dalton laid down covering fire around the entrance, but before Lawrence could reach him a ferocious burst of gunshots came pounding in through the open doorway.

In self-preservation Lawrence skidded to a halt and then leapt through the nearest door into the room in which they had been searching earlier. The gunfire from the front of the saloon petered out, but that appeared to be deliberate when a volley of shots rattled in through the back door.

Dalton glanced over his shoulder and saw men scurrying towards the door with guns brandished. Seeing no other choice, he followed Lawrence in running for the makeshift bedroom. As he slipped into the room, Lawrence slapped him on the back and then the two men considered each other.

'Trapped,' Lawrence said, unhappily.

'And surrounded,' Dalton said.

In the saloon room, footfalls sounded as Cyrus's men moved closer.

9

Dalton and Lawrence hunkered down on either side of the doorway. Then, on the count of three, they edged forward, aiming to pick out targets. But before either man could fire, a rapid volley of shots sliced through the doorway of the room, forcing them to back away.

Dalton slapped the floor in frustration and then, with a sorry shake of the head, he shoved the door closed.

'That won't help none,' Lawrence said.

'Someone'll have to open the door and we can at least make that man suffer,' Dalton said. 'Hopefully, that might give us some time to think of something else.'

Lawrence sighed, but he put aside his misgivings and looked around the room. There were no windows or doors, and so their only chance of finding a way out rested with the unresolved mystery of what lay beneath the raised area.

'You watch the door,' Lawrence said. 'I'll work on this.'

With renewed vigour Lawrence attacked the gap using the broken shovel and he made enough wood splinter away to suggest he would break through. Dalton no longer hoped that he might uncover Thurmond Bryce's treasure, but he did hope that they might find a way out down there.

Beyond the door shuffling sounded as the gunmen got into position, and then Cyrus spoke up.

'You're making a lot of noise in there,' he said. 'These buildings may be in a poor state, but you won't break out.'

Dalton was minded not to respond to the gloating, but he figured that if he could goad Cyrus into acting recklessly that might earn them an advantage.

'We're not looking to break out,' he

called. 'We've found what we came here for.'

Lawrence shot Dalton a bemused look, and so Dalton mouthed that he was trying to buy time. Lawrence muttered in support of this plan and, as it turned out, Cyrus did not respond immediately, thus giving Lawrence enough time to hammer away at the wood until he had created a six-inch-wide hole.

Then he put the shovel aside and stuck the second most useful tool — the crowbar — into the hole. He pivoted downwards and raised the area by several inches along most of its length, accompanied by creaking and snapping sounds.

'So you came back here to steal from us,' Cyrus said, finally. 'You must be desperate.'

'Scavengers can't complain when they get beaten by better scavengers.'

Cyrus snorted. 'Now I know you're lying. What did you really come here for?'

'I'm not explaining nothing to someone who's threatening us.' Dalton waited for Cyrus to take the bait, but he didn't reply. 'All you need to know is that despite knowing you'd got your hands on a crate of guns, we still came back.'

Lawrence slipped the shovel under the gap to keep it open. Then he moved along to a corner where, with the crowbar, he tried to expand the gap along a tighter section.

Near to the door shuffling sounded along with murmured comments, giving Dalton the impression the gunmen were planning to move in — although curiously he also heard someone hurry across the saloon room to the door.

'There's nothing in this town that's worth the risk of taking me on,' Cyrus said, his voice coming from somewhere in the middle of the saloon room.

Lawrence broke off from straining to direct a hopeful glance at Dalton. Then he returned to pressing down on the crowbar and the break had an immediate effect when a loud crack sounded and the raised area flexed along two sides.

'There's nothing you know about, or you'd have found it, but I reckon we can come to a deal here.'

Cyrus murmured to someone and Dalton tried to gauge his mood by the tone of his voice, but the cracking resumed, masking his voice. In a rush the raised area came free and it went swinging upwards until it was some three feet off the floor.

With a reverberating thud the area slammed back down on the floor, landing in a different position than before, showing that it was no longer nailed down. Better still, it revealed a space beneath the floor.

Despite their desperate situation Lawrence and Dalton exchanged intrigued smiles. Then Lawrence got down on his knees and opened up the space so he could peer down.

'There's no way out,' Lawrence

whispered. ''But there's a large chest under here.'

'What are you doing in there?' Cyrus shouted.

'I'll answer that when you accept we can make a deal,' Dalton said as Lawrence pushed the raised area aside to reveal the chest.

With time pressing Lawrence jumped down into the space and swung up the lid. He peered inside and then, with a groan, he leaned over to rummage inside.

'We can't make no deal,' he said, letting the lid thud back down.

Dalton winced and closed his eyes for a moment in disappointment.

'Empty?'

'Worse!' Lawrence kicked the chest and then clambered back on to the floor. 'The only thing in there is a body.'

'Why would there be a . . . ?' Dalton trailed off and then joined Lawrence in groaning. 'Thurmond Bryce, I presume?'

Lawrence waved a document that presumably identified the body.

'Sure — and I presume that means Virgil Tweed followed Thurmond here and killed him.'

The two men faced each other, Lawrence's hunched shoulders confirming that he was as bereft of ideas as Dalton was.

'Make the deal a good one and I'll hear you out,' Cyrus called from the saloon room.

'We might have been allowed to leave town by letting him have the treasure,' Lawrence said. 'But the only thing he'll do now is make sure there's two more bodies in that chest.'

Dalton sighed. Then, with a shrug and a smile, he tried to appear confident.

'Try to convince yourself that this is what we wanted to find.' He raised a hand when Lawrence started to object. 'Then we'll try to convince Cyrus of the same thing.'

He waited until Lawrence provided a

sceptical frown. Then he aimed his gun at the ceiling and faced the door.

Lawrence moved on to join him where he matched his posture. Dalton nodded and then raised his voice.

'We heard about a hidden stash of treasure, Cyrus,' he called. 'We had to come here to confirm where it is. We've done that now.'

Snorts of derision sounded in the saloon room.

'Come out and tell me about it,' Cyrus said, using a sarcastic tone. 'Then you can leave.'

With a deep breath Dalton moved on to the door and kicked it open. Cyrus's men were spread out around the saloon room with their guns trained on the door.

Cyrus stood in their centre with an eager grin on his face, but that didn't deter Dalton from taking a long pace forward.

'The money was found by a man called Thurmond Bryce and he built the Lucky Break saloon.' Dalton paused to let that information sink in and, promisingly, Cyrus nodded. 'Last year Virgil Tweed killed him and dumped his body through there.'

Cyrus glanced past Dalton. 'We never saw that and we've been sleeping in there.'

'If you don't believe me, take a look for yourself,' Dalton snapped, feigning indignation so that the one provable element of his story would sound more convincing.

Cyrus gestured at one of his men, who slipped past Dalton and Lawrence. The man paced across the room and then came out sporting a surprised look.

'The dead man has helped your credibility,' Cyrus said. 'Now explain how that confirms where the money is.'

'You were in Sawyer Creek, so you'll know that Virgil Tweed is a rich man and you'll have heard the rumours that he didn't get his money honestly.'

Dalton didn't know if anyone other than Obediah had doubts about Virgil.

But he figured that, like him, Cyrus had been run out of town after getting into trouble, and it was more than likely that the trouble had happened in the Lucky Break saloon.

'I can believe that Virgil is dishonest.' Cyrus spread his hands. 'So tell me where the money is.'

Dalton matched Cyrus's more casual stance by lowering his gun to aim it down at the floor. Lawrence matched his action, giving Dalton time to think of his response, one that would determine whether they would walk out of the saloon or have to fight their way out.

'It was buried through there, but when Thurmond tried to leave town with it, Virgil claimed it and took the money back to Sawyer Creek.'

Cyrus narrowed his eyes. 'How do you know all this?'

'Because Thurmond's father Obediah Bryce told us.' Dalton sneered. 'He's the man you spiked here yesterday, which means that wasn't the most sensible thing you've ever done as by now he'd have got his hands on the money.'

Cyrus pointed an angry finger at him, and for a long moment Dalton could not tell if his taunt would goad him into violence or make his story sound more valid. Then Cyrus offered a sly smile.

'If Obediah had got to the money quicker, I might not have spiked him.'

Cyrus raised an eyebrow, making a silent but obvious offer and so Dalton nodded.

'We can still get to it.'

'Then do it,' Cyrus snapped, raising his voice so it echoed in the room.

Cyrus stepped to the side and held a hand out indicating the door.

'We will,' Dalton said.

He had not expected he could talk their way out of the situation so easily and so he moved cautiously, giving Cyrus a wide berth as he looked out for deception.

Sure enough, long shadows played on

the ground beyond the saloon door, although when he moved forward he was surprised to see three of Cyrus's men were dragging the shot lawmen to the saloon, presumably acting on Cyrus's loud order. They came in backwards and unceremoniously dumped the bodies in a line before the door.

Dalton had thought the three men had been killed, but the marshal's eyes were open and one of the deputies was murmuring in pain. Cyrus moved over to stand so the bodies were between him and Dalton.

'I believe your story,' he said, 'but if I were to let you go in search of this treasure, you'd flee. But as you're men who saved Obediah's life when you didn't need to, these men are my insurance that you won't run.'

'So what's the deal here, Cyrus?'

Cyrus tapped a boot against the side of the first deputy to be shot, without response, before moving on to repeat the action with the other two lawmen and receive grunted complaints.

'I'll exchange the treasure for these three men.' Cyrus looked along the line of lawmen and smiled. 'One's dead, one's half-dead, and one will die if he doesn't get help soon — so I reckon you should hurry!'

10

It was dark when Dalton and Lawrence rode back into Sawyer Creek. On the back of the wagon was the chest in which they had found Thurmond Bryce's body.

Cyrus had let them leave the saloon with his threats ringing in their ears. He had promised them that unless they returned with the chest filled with money, the lawmen would die. On the way back to town they discussed their options, but they decided that anything they tried would be sure to end badly.

Their only option was to find the money Virgil had stolen from Thurmond Bryce and return it to Randall's Point. Cyrus might still double-cross them, but they would face that problem only if they resolved their first problem.

People were gravitating towards the Lucky Break saloon, but when Dalton and Lawrence left the wagon beside the stable, they headed to the surgery.

As they had no idea what Virgil might have done with the money, they sat down next to the bed of the one man who might have an idea. Unlike earlier, Obediah was agitated and now, worryingly, sweat slicked his brow.

'Don't stay for long,' Wainwright said in a grave tone when Obediah didn't acknowledge them.

'What's wrong with him?' Dalton asked.

'It's too early to be sure, but he could have a fever. That spike couldn't have been none too clean.' Wainwright considered his patient with a sorry shake of the head. 'The next few hours will be crucial.'

'I guess having a metal spike jammed into the guts is about as bad as taking a gunshot,' Dalton said.

'It sure is. Without care any man will probably die; and even with it, he still mightn't survive.'

Wainwright then left them and so

with that sobering thought spurring him on, Dalton leaned over Obediah and ran through the events of the last few hours. Obediah didn't respond, even to the shocking revelation of his son's demise.

'So now that you know your son is lying where the treasure was once buried,' Dalton said, completing the story, 'where do you think the money is now?'

Obediah continued wheezing, appearing as if he hadn't heard the story and that he wouldn't respond, but then slowly he opened an eye and considered Dalton.

'Virgil has it,' he said, quietly.

'We assume so,' Dalton said, patiently, 'but where would Virgil take it?'

'Nobody but us knows about it, so he's kept it secret.'

Dalton waited for more, but Obediah didn't continue. He looked at Lawrence, who shook his head.

'He clearly doesn't know where the stolen money is,' Lawrence said. 'But he's talking sense. For so few people to have even heard about this treasure, Virgil must have dealt with it on his own.'

'And then stamped down ruthlessly on anyone who found anything out,' Dalton said.

They both turned to Obediah, but they got no reply and so Lawrence produced the painting and waved it before Obediah's face in the hope it might make him focus.

'Maybe I shouldn't have stolen this painting,' Obediah said under his breath, as if he were talking to himself as he looked the picture over. 'All that time and effort, and I stole the wrong thing. I should have acted like a man for once. I should have hid in the office and shot up Virgil.'

This line of thought made him murmur in distress and he started twisting around on the bed. Figuring they'd get no help from him, Dalton and Lawrence called Wainwright back into the room.

When the doctor arrived, he shooed them away. Lawrence left the painting beside his bed, and then they did as requested.

At the door Dalton stopped to glance back at Obediah, feeling that this would probably be the last time he saw him alive. Then he joined Lawrence outside.

Lawrence considered the Lucky Break saloon while shaking his head, but Dalton smiled.

'Obediah might not have said much,' he said, 'but I reckon he had the right idea. Virgil was worried about Obediah's intent when he sneaked into his office and he was relieved when he only stole the painting.'

Lawrence nodded. 'So the money must be in his office.'

'That's my assumption.'

'Which only leaves us with the small problem of how we get into an office at the back of a saloon when the owner warned us not to step foot in there again.'

Dalton shrugged and then patted the

wad of bills in his pocket.

'We have money now, so perhaps we should just walk up to the door and go in. He might have forgiven us by now.'

Lawrence laughed and with that optimistic thought they moved on towards the saloon. They timed their approach so that they mingled in with a boisterous group, but any hope that they could slip in unseen fled as the two guards who had followed them yesterday were at the door checking entrants for weapons.

They let everyone in the group enter without delay, but the moment Dalton moved to follow them, the guards closed ranks.

'You know you're not welcome here,' one man said.

'That was yesterday,' Dalton said. 'Today we hoped Virgil might have changed his mind.'

'You two like to push your luck. Go away while you can still walk.'

Dalton figured they had to win this

argument or anything they tried later to get into the saloon would fail, but Lawrence got his attention and beckoned him to give up. Dalton stayed for long enough to tip his hat to the guards, and then joined him in leaving.

'That might have been our best chance to get in,' Dalton said.

'It was about to be our last attempt. One of the guards gave a signal to someone. I reckon reinforcements would have arrived within moments.'

Dalton glanced over his shoulder at the saloon. The guards had returned to checking entrants and they didn't appear to be paying attention to them, but he trusted Lawrence's judgement and so they moved on towards the Double Eagle saloon to discuss their next move.

As they walked both men looked around cautiously, but nobody followed them. They were approaching the saloon and Dalton was starting to think they'd avoided whatever trouble the guards were planning when two men stepped out of the alley beside the saloon.

Dalton and Lawrence stopped, and both groups appraised each other. Dalton reckoned they could best these men and so he nodded to Lawrence, but before they could move off footfalls sounded behind them.

Dalton turned as another two men stepped out of a doorway and, using the element of surprise, these men seized one man apiece. The other two men moved in quickly and in short order they bundled Dalton and Lawrence into the alley and then along it.

Both men struggled and they made their captors fight for every step, but they were moved on inexorably. When they reached the back of the saloon, another two men were waiting for them sporting lively grins and bunched fists.

Lawrence gave Dalton a sorry look that said this was what had happened to him prior to Marshal Walsh running him out of town. Then, with calm efficiency that spoke of the many times these men had meted out punishment, they were disarmed, thrown against the wall, and held securely.

'Virgil gave you a warning,' one man said. 'You ignored it. Now we're giving you a beating. Don't ignore it.'

Dalton tensed in preparation of trying to throw his captor aside, but that encouraged another man to move in on him. With hands pressing against his arms and body, the men combined forces and pinned him to the wall.

Two short-armed punches thudded into his side, but with the men standing close to him they landed without much force and, accordingly, the leader grunted an order to spread out.

Dalton struggled and his captors continued to bustle, but then another man muttered an oath and consternation broke out. A loud crunch sounded that rattled the saloon wall and the men holding Dalton looked away from him.

For a moment the captors parted and let him see that he wasn't causing them problems, but Lawrence was. Urged on by a desire to avoid being beaten again, he was fighting back with berserk energy.

The crunch had come from him throwing off the man who had been holding his arms and then, with his head down, he charged at the leader. He caught this man in the stomach with a leading shoulder and carried him down the alley until the man slipped and went over on to his back.

Lawrence went down with him where he slammed quick punches into the man's side before leaping to his feet to confront the others. Heartened by his success Dalton redoubled his efforts to throw aside his captors.

With Lawrence's success distracting them, he freed his right arm and delivered a swinging punch to one man's jaw that knocked him into the other man. He shoved both men away and then with rapid blows he pummelled anyone he could reach.

He got in four firm punches before

his assailants retaliated by knocking him to the side in an attempt to topple him. Using quick-footed movements he kept his balance.

The leader got to his feet while two men moved purposefully towards Lawrence as they prepared to reverse his initial success.

Dalton reckoned with their superior numbers their captors would probably best him this time, and so he continued moving and used his momentum to slam into the leader's back. The man keeled over and Dalton leapt over his body to join Lawrence, but then he had to jerk aside when Lawrence aimed a wild punch at him.

At the last moment Lawrence checked the punch and offered Dalton an apologetic smile. Then, with a shake of the head, he came to his senses.

'I reckon we've done enough damage,' he said. 'Now, run!'

Dalton took one look at the six men closing in on them and then ran for the widest gap. He barged two men aside and, with Lawrence at his heels, he kept running.

He had reached the back of the saloon before he registered that they were running away from the main drag.

Muttered recriminations broke out behind them and when Dalton looked over his shoulder a straggling line of men was hurrying after them. They were far enough away for Dalton to slow down and let Lawrence draw alongside.

'I don't reckon they're used to anyone fighting back,' Dalton said.

'Then hopefully they'll think twice before attacking us again.'

Dalton liked this optimistic thinking and they took the shortest route back to the main drag. Then they hurried back towards the Lucky Break saloon, figuring that it would be safest to stay in the busiest part of town just then.

By the time the saloon came into sight, the leading bunch of pursuing men were slowing to a halt to let the stragglers catch up with them. The group shared opinions and then moved on slowly.

Dalton figured they were waiting for a suitable moment to accost them again. With most of the people who were outside in the early evening gravitating towards the saloon, it was just a matter of time before the main drag was deserted and they got that chance.

'We can't go in the saloon,' Dalton said, unhappily, 'and we can't stay outside.'

He looked at Lawrence for an idea, but Lawrence shook his head. Then a new man spoke up from the shadows behind them.

'You should follow my lead,' the man said.

Dalton turned to be confronted by the surprising sight of Obediah Bryce walking towards them. He was moving gingerly with an arm pressed across his wounded chest and, despite the evening chill, his brow was damp.

'From the look of you less than an

hour ago, the only place you were going had pearly gates.'

Obediah offered a pained smile. 'I still probably will, but Wainwright gave me something for the pain and that helped me to get out of bed. I figured I might have only the one chance to pay Virgil back for what he did to my son, and I have to take it while I still can.'

'We're obliged for your help. What's your plan?'

'I intend to do the only thing I'm good at,' Obediah said, and with that, he set off for the saloon.

11

With Obediah leading the way at a slow and pained pace, they headed toward the saloon. The guards at the door looked past him to consider Dalton and Lawrence with surprise.

Dalton tipped his hat to them to reinforce the fact that they had not been beaten and so the guards gave Obediah only a cursory glance before closing ranks to bar their way. Obediah stopped and gestured at Dalton and Lawrence.

'They're with me,' he said.

'Then you're barred from the saloon as well,' one guard said.

'My money was good enough the last time I was here.'

One of the guards narrowed his eyes and then whispered to the other. Then they both considered him with bemusement.

'You're the man who was so ill Doctor Wainwright said you probably wouldn't last the day.'

'He could be right, so I'd be obliged if you'd let me enter while I can still stand.'

One guard continued appraising him while the other hurried away. He returned with Virgil Tweed in tow and when Virgil considered the delegation, he matched his guards' bemused expressions before glaring at Obediah.

'If you've come to explain yourself, you can come in,' Virgil said. 'If you haven't, my guards will get that explanation out of you.'

Obediah shrugged. 'I've come to play poker.'

For long moments the two men considered each other until with a small, knowing nod, Virgil stood aside. When Obediah moved on, Dalton and Lawrence followed on close behind before he could change his mind.

Virgil stayed back at the door to whisper instructions to the guards and so Obediah caught Dalton's attention.

'Watch for a distraction,' he said, before moving on to the main poker table where only a few days ago he had cheated Dalton out of everything he had.

As the distraction he had provided that night had been a good one, Dalton beckoned Lawrence to join him at the bar. The guards stayed at the door where one man dealt with newcomers while the other man watched Obediah.

A third guard made his way across the room and stood at the end of the bar, from where he watched Dalton and Lawrence. Only then did Virgil head to the table where he beckoned the players to move aside to let him and Obediah sit.

His action encouraged the customers to turn to the table and so when Obediah gingerly lowered himself into his chair, everyone in the saloon was watching him. Once he was sitting, he breathed a sigh of relief although he kept a hand pressed to his chest.

Virgil gestured for the dealer to give him the cards. Then he dealt them both five cards face down.

'Straight poker, one set of discards?' he asked.

'Agreed,' Obediah said.

'What's the bet?'

'You'll bet everything you took off Thurmond Bryce — my son.'

Virgil flinched back in his chair. 'So that explains your misguided presence here.'

'It does.' Obediah slipped the hand that was pressed against his chest into his jacket and withdrew the folded-over painting. 'And I bet this painting.'

Obediah tossed the picture into the middle of the table where it opened up to reveal a painting that was barely visible through the bloodstains. Virgil glanced at it and then sneered.

'Even if it wasn't worthless, I wouldn't bet everything I own, because you stole this painting off me.'

Obediah shook his head. 'The painting is worthless, but the picture is the

161

most valuable thing my son owned.'

He beckoned Virgil to look at the other side and so with his brow furrowed Virgil drew the painting closer and raised it.

Nearby, customers who had been watching this exchange with lively interest edged forward to see what was so important about the painting, but Virgil slammed it back down on the table before anyone could see the map on the back.

'This would have provided an interesting bet if I didn't know that you're bluffing.'

'I know that, and so my bet is one that my son would approve of, wherever he may be.'

Virgil nodded and leaned back in his chair, his posture acknowledging that he had now worked out that Obediah knew he had got to the treasure and that he had killed his son Thurmond.

'I assume that if I win, I get the painting and its secret?'

'You do. And if I win, I get the

painting's secret.'

This cryptic conversation made the customers bustle and murmur to each other as they edged even closer to the table. Even the guards adopted intrigued expressions, suggesting they didn't know that Obediah had offered to keep the truth that Virgil had killed Thurmond a secret in return for a chance to win Thurmond's fortune.

'Then let's play,' Virgil said.

As the players shuffled up to the table, the customers edged closer to form a ring blocking Dalton's view of them. He craned his neck, but then Lawrence nudged him in the ribs and, when he had got his attention, he beckoned Dalton to join him in slipping into the crowd.

From the corner of his eye Dalton had noted that the guard assigned to watch them had now edged forward to mingle in with the crowd and, although he would glance at them periodically, the poker game held his attention more and more. Dalton glanced at Lawrence, who smiled and so, not questioning their luck, they lowered their heads and then moved cautiously back to the bar.

The guard stayed with the customers while the bartender had moved to the other end of the bar to watch the game, and so Dalton and Lawrence ducked down.

Moving quickly, they shuffled behind the bar with their heads down and then slipped into the corridor that led to Virgil's room. Dalton glanced over his shoulder to confirm nobody was following them and then they hurried on into the office.

Dalton was sure that within a few minutes the guard would notice they had gone, and so they moved around the office quickly as they looked for a safe. After peering under tables and tapping the walls, Lawrence found it in a cupboard in the corner.

The safe was both four feet high and deep, suggesting it was large enough to contain the missing fortune. The combination lock on the door was their next problem, but Lawrence still gave the door a tug before stepping back shaking his head.

'It's too big to move and unless you have a skill you haven't mentioned before, it'd need some of that dynamite Marshal Walsh took to Randall's Point to open it.'

Dalton shrugged and then took hold of the lock.

'I haven't had much luck recently, so maybe it's time for that to change.'

The dial had numbers up to ten and so he turned it to 'five' three times and then all the way round twice.

'Randomly turning the dial won't work. We need a number sequence that means something to Virgil.'

'That was a sequence. When Virgil played Thurmond Bryce at poker, Thurmond won with a full house, fives over tens.'

This line of thinking made Lawrence nod approvingly and then they both smiled before Dalton took the dial again. This time he used Virgil's losing hand of the numbers five through to nine.

With a satisfying click the safe door swung open to reveal neatly stacked rows of bills. While Dalton knelt down to see how far back the money stretched, Lawrence hurried off to search the rest of the cupboards.

The chest that Cyrus wanted them to fill was on the wagon, but thankfully Lawrence found several saddle-bags piled up in a corner cupboard. Within a minute they had emptied the safe and filled three bags.

Dalton hefted a bag finding that it was bulky but not heavy and so, with him hanging a bag over each shoulder and Lawrence taking the other one, they turned their thoughts to escape. The room had no windows and the only door led back to the saloon room.

'Hopefully, Obediah is still distracting everyone,' Lawrence said.

Dalton frowned, but he couldn't see that they had a choice other than to hope their luck held. With Lawrence leading they headed to the door, but they had yet to reach it when rapid footfalls sounded a moment before the guard burst in.

The man turned rapidly as he scanned the room, his furrowed brow showing that he'd only just noticed that they'd gone missing and he was not even sure if they'd be in here.

Lawrence took advantage of his surprise and, with a lithe movement, he swung a saddle-bag off his shoulder and caught the man with a swiping blow to the jaw that knocked him to the side.

Dalton let his saddle-bags drop to the floor to free his arms and he delivered a more substantial punch to the man's cheek that sent him teetering across the room until he slammed into Virgil's desk. He went sprawling over it, and when he righted himself it was to meet two men and two swinging punches that knocked him one way and then the other.

The final blow bent him over and thudded his head into the desk after which he went limp. Dalton wasted no time in confirming the man was unconscious and then he claimed his gun while Lawrence picked up the three bags.

They headed back to the door, but Dalton's fear that someone might have heard the altercation fled when he heard excited chatter in the saloon room. They moved cautiously down the corridor until they came out behind the bar.

'You cheated when you first came into my saloon,' Virgil was saying, his voice rising above the hubbub. 'And you cheated again.'

'You dealt the cards,' Obediah said, his voice low and barely audible. 'How could I have fixed the hands so that I'd win?'

'A thief who stole this painting could find a way.'

'Then you shouldn't have taken my bid in front of all these people.'

Dalton reckoned this was the ideal time to make their entrance and so, with a nod to Lawrence, they moved out from behind the bar.

'As it seems that Obediah won,' Dalton called, 'we'll help him leave with his winnings.'

The customers swung round to face them and so, figuring that moving quickly while being surrounded by people would give them the best chance of brazening this situation out, Dalton and Lawrence moved into their midst.

They made for the door and they were five paces away from it before they emerged from the tight press of customers. The two guards were still at the door and they eyed the saddle-bags draped over Lawrence's shoulders with surprise before their gazes lowered to the gun that Dalton held low.

'You don't get to walk out of here,' one man said.

'I thought poker-players were treated fairly in the Lucky Break saloon,' Dalton said.

He spoke loudly in the hope that the customers might support him in the same way that the prevailing mood had worked against him on his first night here. Sure enough, murmured discontent sounded and, with everyone seemingly happy that they had seen Obediah win a fair game, Virgil spoke up.

'Let them leave,' he said. 'Everyone must know that when they play poker in my saloon, they can be assured of their safety.'

The guards peered at Virgil. Then they both provided knowing nods and stepped aside.

Obediah moved back from the table and with slow paces and his shoulders hunched he headed to the door. Dalton and Lawrence spread apart to flank him and then without catching anyone's eye they headed outside.

When they were standing on the boardwalk, Obediah's strength gave out. He flopped against Dalton, who held him upright until the cool, night air gave him some strength and he righted himself and stood on his own.

'I didn't expect that Virgil would let us leave,' Lawrence said, making Dalton murmur that he agreed.

'He did that only because leaving the saloon was the easy part,' Obediah said. 'Now we have to stay alive for long enough to leave town.'

12

'How did you defeat Virgil when he was the one who dealt the cards?' Dalton asked as they moved away from the saloon.

'I had planned to cheat, but I didn't get the chance,' Obediah said. He laughed. 'As it turned out, I won that hand fairly.'

Lawrence and Dalton both laughed before they turned their thoughts to the serious matter of leaving town with their winnings. They figured that acting quickly was the best plan and so they headed to the stable where they had left the wagon.

Dalton didn't expect they would get far before Virgil's guards followed them, but the first sign of trouble came from the men they'd confronted before going into the saloon. These men had congregated around the wagon and they were leaning back against the sides with casual stances as if they were merely wasting away the evening with idle chatter.

The moment they saw the three men, they stopped talking and spread apart to face them. Dalton slowed down and glanced around for other options, but he saw none.

Few other people were outside to see this confrontation and worse, when he looked over his shoulder, Virgil was now standing in the saloon doorway with his two guards flanking him. Then they moved out on to the boardwalk and walked purposefully towards them.

'We're trapped from both directions already,' Dalton said.

'I can barely walk,' Obediah said. 'Leave me to face Virgil and make a run for it.'

'We're not leaving you.'

'I wasn't offering for your benefit. Virgil wants the money back. My only chance of surviving this is if you run.'

Dalton reckoned he was probably right, but Virgil was closing quickly and, with Lawrence loaded down with the saddle-bags, he doubted they could outrun them. So he moved ahead of the others towards the wagon.

The waiting men closed ranks to confront him, but despite their superior numbers Dalton maintained a strong pace, making them cast cautious glances at each other. Only when Dalton rested his hand beside his holster did they register that he had re-armed himself.

The leader threw his hand to his holster, the men to either side of him following his lead a moment later, but Dalton was already drawing his gun. He blasted a shot into the leader's chest making him keel over before planting a second bullet in the right-hand man's neck.

As this man stumbled into the men nearest the wagon, Dalton turned his gun on the third man. This man had already drawn his gun, but from behind him Lawrence hurled one of the saddle-bags.

Seemingly unsure of the nature of the missile coming towards him, the man flinched away. Even though the bag only thudded ineffectually against his chest, it gave Dalton enough time to slice a shot into the man's side, downing him.

The other men didn't reach for weapons and so Dalton assumed they weren't armed. He aimed at the nearest man and while still advancing he gave him a narrow-eyed look that promised him he had no qualms about dispatching him, either.

The man met his gaze for two paces and then turned on his heel. His capitulation encouraged the other two men to follow him and in short order they moved away from the wagon.

By the time Dalton reached the wagon they were scooting away into town while looking over their shoulders with the same nervous looks that Dalton and Lawrence had provided earlier when they'd been fleeing. When Lawrence joined him he rescued the thrown saddle-bag and threw it and the other two into the back of the wagon.

Obediah was still making his slow way towards them while Virgil was advancing at a pace that would reach him before he reached the wagon. Dalton reloaded quickly and then swung round to face Virgil.

'You made a bet with Obediah,' he said. 'Keep to your side of the bargain and so will we.'

'Bargains are worthless when the participants meet later at the end of a gun.' Virgil chuckled and stopped to let his guards join him. 'That's something Thurmond Bryce learnt the hard way.'

Obediah's step faltered, but he kept moving on.

'Your secret's safe with us,' Dalton said. 'We have no desire to tell Marshal Walsh about it.'

'The marshal is clearing out outlaws from Randall's Point, which means for the moment I deliver justice in Sawyer Creek.'

Obediah stopped his slow journey towards the wagon and with small steps he turned on the spot to face Virgil, who considered him placidly, as if he was prepared to give him one last chance to relent.

'Thurmond's fortune is now mine,' he said. 'You still have the saloon.'

Virgil shook his head and then jerked up a hand. The signal made the guards draw quickly and they both aimed at Dalton, but Dalton had been prepared and so he already had his gun in hand.

He thrust up his gun and slammed a shot high into the chest of the man on the right, downing him. He swung the gun past the unarmed Virgil to aim at the man on the left, but then found that Obediah was in the way.

He couldn't tell if the weak Obediah had stumbled to the side or if he had deliberately placed himself between him and the gunman, but the result was the same. A bullet from Virgil's guard tore into his stomach, making him double over and giving Dalton a clear shot at his shooter.

He fired and his bullet caught the guard in the centre of the forehead, felling him. Dalton stood still while looking around cautiously, but he didn't see anyone else looking their way.

Lawrence followed his lead in glancing around and confirmed with a relieved grunt that the men who had tried to beat them earlier had all fled into the night. Then he hurried on to Obediah.

Dalton kept his gun on Virgil while Virgil glared at him with his upper lip curled back as if promising him that this matter wasn't over. Bearing in mind that the men lying around him had died at Virgil's behest, Dalton was tempted to deliver justice and end Virgil's chance of mounting a reprisal, but by now the gunfight had drawn a crowd of people out of the saloon.

Doctor Wainwright, hurrying from the surgery, was the first to approach them. He waved Lawrence away and knelt over Obediah.

'You don't want to waste all my good work, do you?' he said.

Obediah mustered a smile and Dalton couldn't help but smile, too, as it seemed that every time he'd assumed this man had been killed somehow he'd managed to survive. He moved over to join Wainwright.

'You'll have to stay here while we deal with the money,' he said, kneeling down beside Obediah.

'The doctor will take good ... ' Obediah broke off, his gaze darting up to look past Lawrence.

Dalton looked up to find that Virgil had taken advantage of the distraction to claim a gun off one of his guards. The moment he saw that he'd been noticed he snapped the gun up to aim at the group and, so with little other choice, Dalton fired.

He was kneeling down and so his shot caught Virgil only a glancing blow to the arm giving Virgil enough time to fire. His group was close together and Dalton couldn't tell who Virgil had aimed at, but the shot caught Obediah in the side.

Virgil raised his gun a mite higher, but this time Dalton had him in his sights. He fired and a deadly shot to the chest made Virgil grunt in pain, his gun falling from his hand. Then he fell over to slam down on the boardwalk.

Lawrence hurried over to Virgil. He kicked away the guns Virgil and his men had used and then checked they were dead, leaving Dalton to consider Obediah. But already his eyes were closing and Wainwright was shaking his head.

'I reckon he cheated death enough times for one lifetime,' Wainwright said.

'I reckon he cheated everyone and everything enough times,' Dalton said. 'But I reckon he'll be pleased that Virgil didn't get away with what he did to his son.'

'And I have better news,' Lawrence called. He was leaning over Virgil, who was murmuring something to him.

Lawrence nodded and then moved away from Virgil who, having said whatever it was he wanted to say, flopped down to lie still. Lawrence hurried to Obediah and shooed the other men away so that he could talk to him.

He knelt beside Obediah and whispered something in his ear, and his comment made a brief smile twitch at the corners of Obediah's mouth, giving Dalton hope that he would liven up. But then, with a rattling gasp, his head rolled to the side and Obediah lay quietly on the boardwalk.

Dalton turned to Wainwright, who shook his head and then edged away from them.

'I came to help my patient and I won't stop you from doing whatever it is you're doing,' he said, 'but when Marshal Walsh returns I will tell him what happened here.'

Dalton smiled. 'Actually, now that we have Virgil's undeserved fortune, I hope you'll be prepared to speak to the marshal a lot faster than that.'

Wainwright gave him an odd look, but before Dalton could explain, Lawrence's sorry shake of the head drew his attention.

'We need to reconsider our plans,' Lawrence said, sadly.

Dalton winced. 'Because of Virgil's last words?'

'Sure. They helped Obediah, but they don't help us.' Lawrence pointed at the saddle-bags in the back of the wagon. 'Apparently, the money we took from the safe is counterfeit. It's all worthless.'

13

'Why would the money being fake help Obediah?' Dalton asked when they were a mile out of town.

'It meant his son didn't make the Lucky Break saloon a success only because he found buried treasure in Randall's Point,' Lawrence said. 'He was just a damn fine businessman.'

Dalton glanced into the back of the wagon at Doctor Wainwright, who was sitting between the chest and the saddle-bags filled with worthless money. Despite the perilous situation they were riding into, the doctor had insisted that he join them so he could tend to the lawmen quickly.

Cyrus had ordered them to return alone, but Dalton hoped Wainwright would provide a calming influence on what would surely be a tense confrontation.

'And I guess that means Virgil Tweed was an astute businessman, too, although I don't see why he kept the money.'

'He told me that the money is almost worthless. It came from banks that no longer exist mixed in with good forgeries. Perhaps he hoped he could one day find a use for it — and presumably a dishonest use.'

Dalton nodded and then drew the wagon to a halt.

'In that case, in the dark the bills might look authentic enough to satisfy Cyrus — with a little encouragement.'

Dalton waved the wad of money Obediah had stolen off him. Getting his meaning, Lawrence joined him in clambering into the back.

They opened the chest and emptied the saddle-bags into it. Then Dalton arranged the authentic money on top of the pile of counterfeits so Cyrus would see the good money before he came across the worthless bills.

Wainwright watched them while shaking his head, but he didn't object.

So when they had replaced the lid, they resumed their journey.

They rode in silence and Dalton tried to foster a confident demeanour, figuring that acting as if they believed the money was real would give them their best chance of pulling off the deception.

'What's the plan?' Lawrence asked when the wagon approached the rail tracks.

'I don't have one,' Dalton said. 'I just hope this visit will be third time lucky.'

'And hopefully this will be the third and last time I ever come to this place,' Lawrence said.

Dalton uttered a supportive laugh and then concentrated on watching the scene ahead.

Lawrence's reminder of the previous disastrous visits here made Dalton take a cautious route into town. He took the wagon across the rail tracks earlier than his previous visits and then swung round to head down the centre of the main drag.

As usual Cyrus stayed out of sight, and so Dalton drew up outside the saloon.

'We've completed our side of the bargain, Cyrus,' he hollered. 'It's time for you to complete yours.'

The three men looked at the saloon, but when movement came it was from the station house. A gunman stepped out onto the platform with his gun pointed at the wagon.

His arrival appeared to be the cue for other gunmen to make their presence known. One man moved into the stable doorway and another moved onto the main drag from the mercantile.

Lawrence looked over his shoulder and winced, confirming that gunmen were moving into position behind them, too. When they had been surrounded by a ring of steel, Dalton saw movement in the saloon, but that was only through the gaps in the boards over the windows.

'You're armed and I reckon you're preparing to deceive me,' Cyrus said from behind the door. 'Put those thoughts from your mind, or you and your lawmen friends won't leave here alive.'

'You're hiding in there and looking as if you're preparing to deceive us,' Dalton said levelly. 'Put those thoughts from your mind, or I'll make sure you don't enjoy Thurmond Bryce's hoard.'

'I'm pleased we understand each other.'

Dalton didn't wait for Cyrus to provide instructions on how the trade-off would proceed, figuring that taking the lead would ensure it developed in the safest way for them. He beckoned Wainwright to get down off the wagon and then he and Lawrence clambered into the back.

Wainwright let down the tailboard and Dalton shoved the chest to the edge of the wagon. They still had the makeshift stretcher made from two spikes and a sack that they had used to move Obediah, and thus they dragged the chest on to the sack.

Dalton looked at the saloon. He detected movement inside and a few moments later a man came through the doorway supporting Marshal Walsh. The marshal struggled to walk and so he had to be dragged across the boardwalk.

Wainwright moved towards him, but Cyrus followed them out of the saloon and waved a warning hand at him to stay back. Then he glanced at the treasure chest before fixing his gaze on Dalton's gun.

Although he hated being powerless he had to admit that they were surrounded and whether he had a gun or not, if he chose to, Cyrus could cut him down within moments. Moving slowly he tipped out the gun on to the ground, as did Lawrence.

Cyrus beckoned them to back away from the guns. Then he directed his man to take the marshal around the wagon.

When he was facing Dalton, the man

stopped and released Walsh, who, without support, dropped to his knees. Nevertheless, the marshal defiantly raised his head to provide Dalton with a brief smile.

'The other man now,' Dalton said.

'He didn't make it,' Cyrus said as he moved along the side of the wagon to join the others. 'You clearly weren't quick enough.'

'And you clearly didn't take good enough care of him. I hope — '

'Dalton,' Walsh muttered, interrupting him. 'I don't want to spend my last moments listening to you two posturing.'

Dalton nodded. Then he slapped the lid of the chest and faced Cyrus.

'I'll hand over the money and at the same time you'll hand over the marshal. Then we can both move on.'

'We'll do that,' Cyrus said, 'but you don't get to move on straight away. The marshal can leave on the wagon with the doctor, but you'll stay here, for now.'

Dalton had not intended to use the wagon to pursue Cyrus as Wainwright needed to get Walsh back to town quickly, but if that was Cyrus's main concern he saw no reason to argue. He nodded to Lawrence and they jumped down from the wagon.

They gripped the spikes on either side of the chest and the gunman drew Walsh to his feet. So they swung the stretcher down and deposited the chest on the ground in front of the advancing men before throwing the spikes back into the wagon.

Then they stepped away from the chest and held out their arms to take control of the marshal. The gunman passed Walsh to them without comment and then moved on to the chest.

Dalton stopped looking out for deception and, with Lawrence's help, they led Walsh to the wagon. Wainwright moved in and gave Walsh a cursory glance before declaring him fit enough to travel.

By the time they had worked out how

to get him on to the back of the wagon, the gunman had opened the chest. His whoop of delight was enough to convince Cyrus that he had got what he wanted and so, when Dalton raised the tailboard, he had hurried on to join the gunman in counting the wads of bills inside.

'There's more than enough for you in there,' Dalton said, hoping to distract Cyrus before he examined the contents too carefully.

Cyrus removed a wad and waved it at Dalton.

'Your wagon can leave,' he said. 'You'll stand there where I can watch you.'

Wainwright didn't need any further encouragement and, with a glance at Dalton, who offered him a brief smile, he hurried around to the seat. Within moments the wagon was heading out of town.

On the back, Walsh raised himself on to an elbow to glare at Cyrus, warning him that this matter wouldn't end here.

But Cyrus didn't notice as he enjoyed the sight of all the money in the chest. So Walsh flopped back down on his back and, as Dalton watched the wagon leave town, he didn't raise himself again.

When the wagon moved out of sight beyond the last building, he turned to Lawrence and, without discussion, they backed away from Cyrus.

They were still surrounded by gunmen, but Dalton figured that avoiding Cyrus as best as they were able would give them their best chance of avoiding another confrontation.

Dalton assumed that Cyrus had horses nearby. Sure enough, when he had enjoyed gloating over the money, Cyrus ordered the man who had brought Walsh out of the saloon to head out of town and fetch them. Then he considered Lawrence and Dalton.

'You did well,' Cyrus said. 'I can see that giving you the motivation of saving someone's life inspired you to do the right thing.'

Dalton shrugged, avoiding this obvious attempt to provoke them, and then glanced at the chest.

'Now that you're pleased with the result, are you going to show your gratitude?'

Cyrus chuckled and then glanced over Dalton's shoulder. The lively gleam in his eye made Dalton tense a moment before a gunshot rang out.

He turned quickly to find that the man in the stable doorway had fired the gun. Then Lawrence groaned and stumbled to the side, showing him who the target had been.

As Lawrence dropped to one knee while clutching his bleeding thigh, Dalton moved closer and grabbed his shoulders, stopping him from falling over.

'I hope that's enough gratitude,' Cyrus said. 'I had planned to shoot you both.'

'Why?' Dalton murmured. 'We did everything you asked and we weren't planning to double-cross you.'

'As with the marshal, saving your friend's life will make you keep your side of the bargain. By the time you've got Lawrence back to Sawyer Creek, we'll be long gone.'

Dalton started to snap back a retort, but even with his support Lawrence pressed against him as he struggled to stay upright. His leg was bleeding profusely and so, acting quickly, Dalton let him drop to the ground.

He ignored Cyrus as he removed Lawrence's belt and wrapped it around his upper leg. With a quick lunge he tightened the belt as strongly as he could, making Lawrence screech in pain, but within moments his actions had stemmed most of the bleeding.

Dalton looked out of town, but the wagon had gone and Lawrence looked to be in too much pain to walk any distance. He reckoned he would have to come up with another way to move him, as he had planned to do with Obediah Bryce, so his first priority was to let Lawrence rest for a while.

The nearest building was the saloon and so he got Lawrence's attention and pointed at it. Lawrence mustered a weak nod and then with a deep breath he raised a hand for Dalton to help him move.

Dalton slipped a hand around Lawrence's waist and Lawrence gripped his shoulder, but when he raised him Lawrence didn't have the strength to hold on and he slipped back down to the ground.

Cyrus laughed at their predicament, but when they ignored him and tried again, he gestured in all directions to his men. From the corner of his eye Dalton noted that the gunmen moved from their positions around town, so presumably the man who had left to fetch their horses would arrive soon.

On the second attempt Dalton raised Lawrence on to his one good leg. Then they took slow and faltering steps towards the saloon.

They managed four steps before Lawrence stumbled to the side, taking

Dalton with him, after which he halted and stood upright.

'Just take a moment and we'll try again,' Dalton said.

'I'm not resting,' Lawrence whispered. 'I'm only one more step away from our guns.'

Dalton glanced down to see that Lawrence had been right. The guns were lying near Lawrence's feet. If Lawrence stumbled in that direction again, he should be able to claim one of them, but instead he gathered a firmer grip of Lawrence's waist.

'Cyrus has done his worst. We just need to get you to safety now.'

'If he examines the money carefully, do you trust him not to do anything else to us?'

Lawrence gave Dalton a long look and in response Dalton nodded. Then Lawrence flexed his good leg and took a cautious pace forward before stumbling to the side again, this time deliberately.

Dalton released his hold to let Lawrence drop down on to his good knee while looking around for the guns. One gun was another pace away and the other was beneath Lawrence's leg that he was holding out awkwardly.

Dalton resisted the urge to check he wasn't being watched as this would only make their activities look suspicious, and he bent over for the nearest gun. His outstretched fingers were inches from the weapon when gunfire rattled.

Lawrence slumped against him. Dalton couldn't support his weight and they both went down on their sides, falling away from the guns.

'I knew you'd try to double-cross me,' Cyrus said from behind, his tone animated.

Lawrence had fallen over Dalton's right arm, ensuring he couldn't even try to reach the gun. Dalton struggled to roll him aside and then with a heavy heart he noted Lawrence's glazing eyes.

He glanced down and confirmed Lawrence had been shot again and this time he had been holed in the chest.

With his free hand Dalton shook Lawrence, but there was no response.

Dalton lowered his head in apparent resignation, but he used the motion to flex his trapped arm and then draw it free.

He was ten paces from the saloon doorway and even though gunmen were moving in from either side, they wouldn't be able to intercept him before he reached the doorway. He put his freed hand to the ground and moved for the gun, making Cyrus fire.

The slug sliced into the hardpan between Dalton and the gun, but Dalton's attempt had been only a feint. He withdrew his hand and kicked off from the ground.

Then, with his head down, he ran for the saloon. Gunfire kicked at his heels and Cyrus chortled with delight, letting him know that he was toying with him, but Dalton didn't mind if it let him reach a place where he could shelter.

He pounded across the boardwalk before throwing himself through the doorway. Then he skidded to a halt and confirmed that he was the only one in the saloon room.

He skirted around the wall so that he wouldn't be seen through the doorway, but even before he had reached the back door, he saw that it had been blocked off.

He figured that by the time he had torn away the wood that had been placed over the door, Cyrus would have sent men round to the back to intercept him.

Even if he could get out that way, there was nowhere close by he could hole up.

He turned away from the door, deciding his best chance was to stay here and, if Cyrus wanted to kill him, someone would have to come inside to do it.

Accordingly, he searched for the best place to hide, noting that the bar offered the only substantial cover. Then, following his policy of trying to second-guess Cyrus, he picked a less

199

obvious place to go to ground.

The boards that had been covering the doorway had been dropped beside the door and so he propped them up over the remnants of a broken table. Then he hunkered down behind them.

To be effective he would have to move quickly the moment anyone came through the door, and so he settled his weight on his toes. Long moments passed without Cyrus making a move, although he heard a wagon trundling closer.

Dalton couldn't hear anyone close to the saloon and so he risked glancing through a gap in the boards over the window. Lawrence was lying where he had fallen while Cyrus was standing over the chest with his men lined up to either side.

Only two men were casting casual glances at the saloon while the rest watched the wagon draw up. Almost as if Cyrus had detected Dalton's bemusement, he turned to the saloon.

'You'll have seen by now that I

blocked off the back door,' Cyrus called. 'Now you'll be wondering what I have in store for you.'

For several moments Cyrus faced the saloon, but when it became clear that he had not goaded Dalton into replying, he shrugged and nodded to the nearest gunman.

This man raised his gun to aim at the saloon, although as he was aiming at a spot several yards from where Dalton was standing, Dalton didn't take cover and he continued to watch him.

The man fired, the shot slamming into the saloon wall. Then he fired twice in rapid succession.

The other gunmen laughed and with good cheer they slapped each other on the back while encouraging the shooter, who settled his stance and fired again.

He shook his head and this encouraged the other men to raise their guns. Intrigued now, Dalton moved position so that he could see down the length of the wall.

When he saw what they were aiming

at, Dalton couldn't help but wince.

The sticks of dynamite with which Walsh had planned to destroy the saloon were still where he had left them. They were lying on the board-walk — and the gunmen were taking aim at them.

14

Dalton watched a gunshot make a stick of dynamite kick up into the air without mishap, and then he groaned as he saw how it fell back down, propped up against a corner post, giving the gunmen a clear shot at the fuse.

He counted three other sticks lying along the front of the saloon. Dalton reckoned lighting a fuse this way would be hard, but the gunmen were enjoying their sport and, if they tried for long enough, one of them was sure to get lucky.

'Keep firing!' Cyrus shouted. 'When we leave, I want everyone in Sawyer Creek to see this place burn.'

The gunfire increased in intensity as everyone joined in. The gunmen spread out as they adopted a variety of angles and, with their attention all being on the dynamite, Dalton noted the position of the two guns lying beside Lawrence's body.

He figured that he wouldn't cover even half the distance before the gunmen transferred their attention on to him, and so he gathered up two of the boards and held them together.

The makeshift shield wouldn't deflect the bullets, but it would mask his exact position.

He waited until there was a lull in firing, hoping this would be when several men were reloading, and backed away from the door for several paces to get a run-up. Then, with his head down, he set off at speed so by the time he surged through the door he had already built up a decent pace.

In two strides he left the boardwalk and embarked on the ten paces that would get him to the guns. He covered the first three paces before gunfire erupted and then, to his delight, from the corner of his eye he saw that the target had still been the dynamite.

Another two shots tore out before someone fired at him. The shot tore through the wood a few inches from his right ear, making him flinch away — an action that saved him when two more shots sliced through the wood grouped around that spot.

Dalton figured the next round was sure to at least wing him and so, with a roar of effort, he hurled the boards towards the gunmen. Two more shots clattered into the boards while they still blocked his view of the gunmen, and then they tumbled end over end, revealing the men along with the guns lying ahead.

Dalton lowered his head until he was so doubled over that he was in danger of falling, and then he dived to the ground. He slid along the dirt on his stomach with his arms outstretched as he reached for the nearest gun, but as he closed on it an accurate shot from one of the gunmen skittered the gun away to the side.

When Dalton came to rest both guns

were still out of reach and so he moved to get up and leap again, but then found that Cyrus had trained his gun on him and he was shaking his head.

'Get back to the saloon,' Cyrus said. 'I want to see you die in there.'

Dalton rolled his shoulders as he prepared to leap towards the gun anyhow, but then he saw movement behind Cyrus. He looked away before Cyrus noticed his surprise and fixed Cyrus with his firm gaze.

'I got bored sitting around in there waiting for your men to hit the fuse,' he said.

'They'll hit one just as soon as you move back to where you belong.'

Dalton shook his head. 'They clearly don't know how to use dynamite. Perhaps you need a demonstration from someone who knows what they're doing.'

Cyrus sneered, thankfully not understanding Dalton's taunt, although unfortunately Dalton's timing proved to be poor as long moments then dragged on in silence. Cyrus jutted his jaw, his patience clearly reaching its limit until, with a shake of the head, he raised his gun slightly to aim it at Dalton's chest.

Then the station house blew up.

Dalton had been prepared for this to happen and so he shook off his shock quickly and leapt for the gun. He gathered up the weapon, rolled over a shoulder, and then used his momentum to gain his feet.

He put aside any thoughts of launching an immediate assault on Cyrus and his men and, while they were still shocked by the unexpected turn of events, he ran for the saloon.

Prior to the blast he had seen Marshal Walsh shuffling out of the station house and making his way to the mercantile, leaving behind several sticks of fizzing dynamite. Dalton had hoped the lawman would then launch an assault on Cyrus's men, but he now remembered that Walsh had bought sufficient dynamite to destroy the whole town.

Only some of it was set out before the saloon and, as the blast in the station house had not been massive, he might have other surprises in store. Dalton reached the saloon without reprisals and then hunkered down inside the door.

Cyrus was obviously unaware that only one man had launched an attack on him as he gathered his men by the newly arrived wagon where they hunkered down and looked in all directions.

Dalton added to his woes by firing a couple of quick shots. They both clattered into the back of the wagon, but they made the gunmen scurry around the other side, which placed them in Walsh's firing line.

Several men peered over the top of the wagon at the saloon and so before they could fire at him, Dalton hammered rapid shots that sliced into the wood, forcing them to drop down. Then he slipped away from the door and into the saloon.

While he reloaded gunfire rattled, but he didn't hear the shots hitting the saloon. When he looked through the door, it was to find that Walsh had made his presence known.

Gunfire reports came from a window in the mercantile, and Walsh had picked his targets well as first one man and then another threw up their arms in pain before dropping to the ground.

Cyrus shouted orders and the rest of his men went to their knees and then scurried along beneath the wagon to get away from Walsh's gunfire. They didn't emerge on the other side and instead took the only available cover of the wheels.

Some men lined up to face Dalton and the others faced Walsh, suggesting that they had now worked out these were the only directions from which they might get attacked. Dalton didn't think it likely that Doctor Wainwright would have returned along with Walsh, so he concentrated on working with

Walsh to keep the gang pinned down.

So, when Walsh stopped firing Dalton laid down steady gunfire at the wagon, and the moment he stopped Walsh started firing. He and the lawman both had cover that was more effective than the wagon and, after trading gunfire for another minute, Dalton hit a target for the first time.

He slammed lead into one man's shoulders, making him roll to the side and, with a clearer target, he dispatched the injured man with a shot to the head.

This had an unexpected result when a gunman edged out from beneath the wagon to drag back his dead associate, giving Dalton a clear target. Dalton sliced lead into this man's chest, dropping him without effort.

After that success the others stayed down and, with them not returning fire, Walsh and Dalton both held their fire.

A tense stand-off ensued with neither side making an aggressive move. After several minutes Cyrus gathered his men's attention and, with muttered comments and gestures, they clearly hatched a plan.

The result of these deliberations came when two men swapped positions behind the wheel nearest to the saloon. One man adopted a position where Dalton couldn't see him and, when he fired, Dalton flinched away from the door.

Dalton didn't hear where the shot landed and, as he didn't think he was the target, he moved back into the doorway. When the man fired again, Dalton saw that he was aiming at a stick of dynamite that was lying propped up against the corner post with the fuse prominent.

The man continued to fire at regular intervals and it was clear that he was aiming carefully. Dalton could see splinters kick up as the gunman closed in on his target.

Dalton still didn't think the gunman would be able to ignite the fuse and he figured if Cyrus's plan was to wait until the gunman succeeded before he fled in the ensuring chaos, his best course of action was to avoid panicking and to sit it out.

Two shots later the fuse ignited.

The success was clearly unexpected as the gunman fired again and several moments passed before another gunman whooped with delight. Cyrus got everyone's attention and then, in a surge of movement, they came up from under the wagon.

Two gunmen stood together to hammer lead at the mercantile while another two men joined ranks to fire at the saloon doorway. While Cyrus directed operations from beneath the wagon, the last man hurried for the wagon seat.

Walsh fired at the wagon, but before Dalton could help him, lead peppered around the doorframe. Dalton jerked backwards and pressed his back to the wall.

From his position he couldn't see the wagon, although he heard Cyrus urging everyone to act on his orders and he could see the fizzing fuse. He judged that he had around thirty seconds.

Running to the back of the saloon would get him to safety, but only if the blast didn't ignite the rest of the dynamite lying along the front of the saloon.

Ten seconds of his remaining time had elapsed when the volley of lead being directed at the saloon died out. So Dalton kicked off from the floor and, with his head held low, he ran out from the saloon along the boardwalk.

He had covered half the distance to the dynamite before the gunmen started firing. The lead clattered into the saloon wall and then the boarded window behind him.

The sounds were getting closer and so, three paces from the corner post, Dalton dived. He hit the boardwalk on his chest, slid along, and with an outstretched hand he gathered up the dynamite. Then, as fast as he was able, he scrambled past the corner post to kneel down on the hardpan.

He had planned to turn the tables on his opponents by throwing the dynamite at the wagon and, when he drew back his arm, he saw that the wagon had started rolling. But Walsh had sown confusion amongst Cyrus's men.

The two gunmen who had faced the mercantile were lying face down in the dirt and the men who had been firing at the saloon were skirting around the back of the wagon. Cyrus was running across the main drag for the chest containing the money and so, making a quick decision, Dalton hurled the dynamite at the chest.

The fuse spluttered in the night air, looking like a shooting star as it rose up and then dropped down towards the chest. Cyrus kept running until at the last moment he saw that the throw would be accurate.

Cyrus skidded to a halt and then pounded back towards the wagon. He had yet to reach it when Dalton judged that the blast was imminent and he hugged the dirt.

A moment later Thurmond Bryce's fortune lost the last of its value.

When Dalton looked up the chest had been obliterated and the most expensive fire Dalton had ever seen was raging. As the burning bills spread out in all directions, Cyrus stared at them in horror before, with an angry shake of the head, he turned round to face Dalton.

Dalton got up on his haunches while swinging his gun up, but before he could take aim, Cyrus fled. He disappeared behind the wagon, passed the two gunmen who were now eyeing the mercantile, and joined the driver on the seat.

Walking sideways Dalton edged away from the saloon. He along with Walsh had taken a heavy toll on Cyrus and he now had only three gunmen.

The two standing men glanced at their colleagues' bodies and, as the wagon lurched to a start, with resigned shrugs they appeared to accept that retreat was the most sensible course of action. They hurried round to the back and with lithe movements vaulted into the wagon.

From the mercantile Walsh fired at them, but his shots clattered into the side of the wagon and they didn't goad the men into raising themselves. Dalton moved on to stand behind the wagon to watch it leave town, but after only a dozen turns of the wheels Cyrus took the reins and swung the wagon around.

Dalton stopped and trained his gun on the wagon as he waited to get a clear view of Cyrus. Despite everything that had happened, he resolved to let him leave if he took the wagon towards the rail tracks, but once the wagon faced the station house, Cyrus continued to turn it.

As the wagon surged past the ruined station house, the two gunmen rose up from the back to fire at the mercantile. Walsh fired back and with his second shot he caught one of the men in the side, making him stumble to his knees.

A second shot made him keel over to lie over the tailboard before he tumbled down to the ground. The second man ducked down and then scurried to the back where as Cyrus continued to turn the wagon he faced the mercantile.

Dalton then stopped waiting to get a clear shot at this man as it became clear that Cyrus was directing the wagon towards him. He edged away from the saloon while moving lightly on his feet, and within moments the horses faced him.

With alarming speed they bore down on him, but Dalton continued to move away from the saloon. When he was sure Cyrus had committed himself to a course, he dug in a heel and ran in the opposite direction.

Even so, the horses loomed over him and he had to leap aside to avoid them. He rolled twice and came to rest on his back, only to be confronted by the sight of a gunman leaping off the seat with his arms spread so that he could pin him to the ground.

With a jerk of his shoulders Dalton bucked himself from the ground while twisting, and he managed to roll onto his side, leaving the man to slam to the ground on his chest with a pained grunt. Dalton gained his feet and looked up at the other gunman, who was training his weapon on him over the back of the wagon.

The man fired, but Cyrus was slowing the wagon down and that made him jerk around. The shot sliced into the ground at Dalton's feet, but Dalton had no such problem and, with his feet planted firmly on the ground, he trained his gun on the man's chest and fired.

The slug hit its target with deadly accuracy, making the man flinch upright before he stumbled and tipped over the side of the wagon. Dalton then turned back to the other man, who was on the point of getting up and freeing his gun arm.

He didn't even get to aim at Dalton as Walsh dispatched him from the mercantile with an accurate shot that sliced into his forehead.

And that left only Cyrus.

The wagon was coming to a halt at the back of the stable and even though Dalton couldn't see Cyrus, he trained his gun on the seat. Without checking he figured Walsh would be doing the same and, bearing in mind the lawman's accuracy, Dalton wasn't surprised when Cyrus stayed down low.

A minute passed and with Cyrus still not making a move, Dalton walked towards the back of the wagon. He didn't reckon Cyrus could have moved away from the wagon without either himself or Walsh noticing. Even so, the wagon had stopped in an area where the light was poor.

Dalton narrowed his eyes as he looked for even the slightest movement and when he detected nothing he stopped two paces away from the back. He waited and a creak broke the silence, alerting him a moment before

Cyrus loomed up, clutching another murderous spike.

Cyrus hurled the spike down at Dalton and only the earlier warning ensured Dalton reacted quickly. He leapt aside, but the spike still sliced down into the ground so close to him that he felt the metal brush his hip.

He landed on his knees where he shook off his shock and then looked up to find Cyrus leaping down from the wagon at him. With only a moment to act, he reached for the spike and it came to hand.

Cyrus hit him, sending Dalton sprawling on to his back. While he gathered his breath Dalton looked up at Cyrus's snarling expression.

He put a hand to Cyrus's shoulder and tried to push him aside, but he couldn't move him. Then he noticed Cyrus's fixed and glazed expression.

With a groan of disgust Dalton saw that when he had grabbed the spike he had raised it just high enough for Cyrus to impale himself on it. Like Abraham on the night that his battle with Cyrus had begun, the spike had entered his chest and it was now poking out of his back.

'That was for Abraham, Lawrence and all the rest,' Dalton said in Cyrus's ear.

Cyrus snarled as he breathed out. He did not breathe in again.

15

'Obliged that you came back to help me,' Dalton said.

'Doctor Wainwright wasn't pleased about it,' Marshal Walsh said through gritted teeth. 'But when I heard the shooting I had to do whatever I could. At least now I'll never again have to worry about people holing up here.'

Dalton nodded. When he had joined Walsh to offer his thanks, one of the burning bills from the chest had reached the saloon and then moved on to set light to the dynamite.

In an instant the saloon had been destroyed and by the time they had started to move down the main drag, the flames had reached the next-door stable.

Dalton judged that with many of the buildings being close together, most of the town would burn down tonight.

He looked to the edge of the circle of light cast by the flames. The doctor had stopped the wagon on the edge of town because the horses would not move any closer.

Cyrus's horses had bolted in the other direction, so he offered Walsh his hand, but Walsh waved him away.

Walsh then embarked on a slow and faltering walk. Dalton reckoned that if he could walk he would be fine and so he hurried back to Lawrence.

His friend lay where he had fallen and the heat blasting out from the saloon meant he couldn't move him in any dignified way. So he grabbed his shoulders and dragged him backwards.

Once he was away from the worst of the heat he hoisted his friend up to a standing position and, with Lawrence's feet dragging along the hardpan, he followed Walsh. The marshal's pace was slow, so he moved past him and Wainwright hurried on to meet him.

Sadly, with only a quick glance, the doctor declared Lawrence beyond his help. Then he moved on to Walsh, who was beginning to stagger, and this time the lawman didn't refuse the offer of help.

At the wagon Dalton hoisted Lawrence's body up on to the back and then stood back. By the time Walsh and Wainwright arrived, he had decided that he had had enough of Sawyer Creek and so he wouldn't be returning to town with them.

He helped Walsh up onto the back. Then he tipped his hat to him and Wainwright.

'I'll be moving on now,' he said. 'The train's due tomorrow morning and I'm overdue to be on it.'

Walsh offered him a pained look, but now that he had completed his duty he was struggling to stay conscious. He accepted Dalton's decision with a quick nod before lying down in the wagon.

Wainwright wasted no time in clambering up onto the seat and in short order he moved on. Dalton watched them go.

Then he turned back to the burning town, figuring with a rueful smile that he would probably enjoy a warmer evening than his first night here. He watched the flames, trying to judge which building was the most likely to stay intact.

Before he could make a decision, movement at the edge of his vision caught his attention and, when he turned to it, an object fluttered across the ground. As it passed, he trapped it beneath a boot and he smiled when he saw that it was a dollar bill.

The bill was singed around the edges, but he judged that it was still intact enough to be valid, provided it was one of the legal ones.

'Everyone connected to Thurmond Bryce's treasure has either left town or is dead,' he said to himself as he pocketed the bill. 'So I guess this treasure is now all mine.'

He looked into town and noted other fluttering bills. Most of them were burning or had already burnt to ash, but he moved on into town to search for more.

By midnight, he had salvaged a small pile and by the light of the burning town he had picked out several that he reckoned were legal tender. When he got to wherever the train would take him, these few dollars would be enough for a meal and a couple of whiskeys.

He figured the rest were helping to keep him warm.